The Darby Crime Family Book One

International Bestselling Author
Jewelz Baxter

Credits:
Model: Johnny Baxter
Photographer: Tim Spillers Photography
Cover Design: CT Cover Creations
Edited: Rebecca Vazquez / Dark Syde Books
Formatted: Jewelz Baxter

Kiss of Power, 1st Edition Copyright 2023 by Jewelz Baxter,

Leather Pinion Publishing LLC

All rights reserved. This book or any portion thereof may not be reproduced or used in any manner whatsoever without the express written permission of the publisher except for the use of brief quotations in a book review. This is a work of fiction. Names, characters, places, and incidents are either the product of the author's imagination or are used in a fictional manner. Any resemblance to actual persons, living or dead, or actual events is entirely coincidental.
www.authorjewelzbaxter.com

ISBN: 978-1-961212-00-8

Author's Notes

~Disclaimer~

Each edition of the Mayhem Makers series includes scenes incorporating the Motorcycles, Mobsters, and Mayhem Signing into their stories. Although the book signing is an actual event, none of the occurrences mentioned in the books are real. They are only part of each author's imagination.

~Warning~

This book contains adult themes such as offensive language, violence, and graphic sexual content. Note there are scenes of dubious consent that some readers may find disturbing. The book is only appropriate for adult readers age 18+.

Dedication

For all who
Kiss the silent monsters
walking among us.

You are the special ones for seeing
what truly lies hidden beneath
their forced mask
of Power.

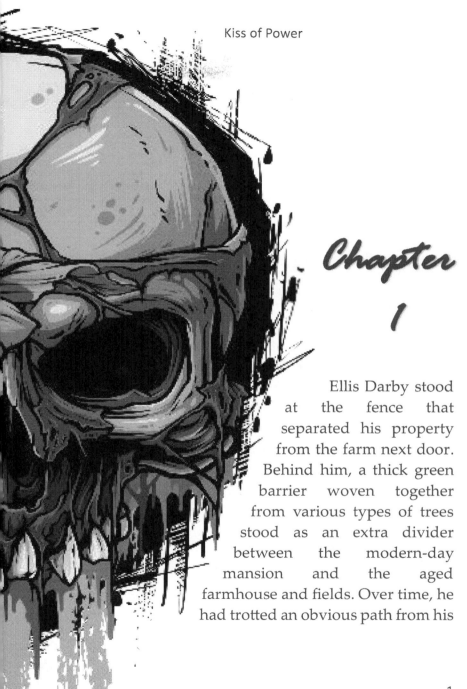

Chapter 1

Ellis Darby stood at the fence that separated his property from the farm next door. Behind him, a thick green barrier woven together from various types of trees stood as an extra divider between the modern-day mansion and the aged farmhouse and fields. Over time, he had trotted an obvious path from his professionally landscaped yard through the maze of trees to this spot.

Positioned in the shadows of the satsuma trees that grew just beyond the fence line, he had remained undetected. The trees filled one corner of the pasture that his neighbor's daughter was strolling through.

She was a sight to behold. One he took pleasure in admiring at every opportunity. Some might call her buxom. Ellis called her perfect. An hourglass shape with an hour and half worth of sand, ample on the top and on the bottom. Beautiful and feisty. What he considered a perfect combination.

Arabella Bartel was twelve years his junior. She was just a tike when he was a teenager throwing hay for her father, and she was constantly getting in the midst of things. By the time he returned home from college, she was becoming a teenager and was rarely seen. As time went on, and by the time Ellis's father passed and he returned to take over his childhood home, she had moved out on her own.

Surprisingly, one day a little over a year ago, Ellis happened upon the stunning spitfire during a daily stroll. Covered in dust, she'd straightened from a blackberry vine that traveled along a fence, catching him off guard as he passed. She'd swiped the back of her hand across her face and blew a whisp of dark hair from her lips. The instant her gaze fell on him, she chastised him for staring, then proceeded to explain that she'd moved back to care for her mother and help her father. She also made it intently clear that he was not welcome on their property. While she was away, she had heard the stories of how his family had raped the town of small business owners unwilling to bow to their demands. And she would resort to any means necessary to keep their land from his clutches.

Her spirited threats had done nothing but intrigue him. He wished her luck in avoiding him and carried on with his walk, knowing this route had, in that moment, gained importance.

He smiled at the memory and watched as she moved closer. Her and that bull of hers. It seemed to make every step she did, lumbering close behind. Ellis stepped into the morning sun. "Most have dogs that trail behind."

"Not as fun." She stopped a few feet from the fence and stroked the bull's neck. "Burger King is special." Her glare narrowed on him. "Why are you here anyway?"

Ellis stretched his neck, viewing the length of wire dividing the properties. "Checking your fence line."

She crossed her arms over her bright tee that was the same color as the fruit next to them. "So you can sneak in and harass the animals?"

"To assure your bovine stays off my property."

"Burger King has no desire to step one hoof onto your snooty land."

He cocked his head, his gaze dropping to the dust-covered boots that hid the bottom of her well-fitting jeans before sliding back up to her eyes. "Unlike you?"

Her eyes widened. "I do not."

He twisted and leaned back, studying the fullness of the trees. "I see someone harvested satsumas recently."

"So," she snapped and returned to pampering the animal when he nudged her arm.

He stepped closer to the fence, drawing her attention to the nearest trees. "The limbs of these two hang over the fence."

"So, you steal them?"

"Technically, they are on my property, so you're trespassing to get them."

"I do not set foot on your precious ground."

"You shimmy the tree to pluck them by hand?"

"They're cut at the stem. And I use a ladder."

"Trespasser." He stretched and plucked a bright orange orb.

"Thief!"

Ellis tugged the peel, breaking it open. "Prove it." He popped three wedges of the citrus into his mouth to experience an explosion of juices. "Hmm . . . sweet." He turned to walk away and swore he could feel her stare burning straight through him, though he restrained from glancing back to confirm that fact. Separating another chunk of wedges, he savored the early morning treat as he strolled back toward his home.

***

Later that day, Ellis sat on his balcony. He focused on the bare gaps in the woodland that spring was bringing back to life and surveyed the land blending into the horizon. Land he intended to control.

It was a family-owned farm that appeared odd and out of place next to the mansion from where Ellis studied it. But it was what it was. Each homestead had been handed down from father to son throughout generations, both growing in size. His grew more lavish. The farm spread wider.

Before Ellis's father passed, he had recommended—no, he had demanded—the family move on to a larger city. His father said they'd squeezed all they could from this little community, so they must spread their wings and dig talons into larger prey.

Ellis had remained by his father's side, along with his brothers, forging the Darby empire until their father's last breath. That's when he returned here. He felt the community still had a lot to give and planned to spread his kingdom as the Bartels had. Outward. By taking one community after the other, he would in time rule the region.

And how fortunate was it that only days before this, Bartel had requested an audience with Ellis. A smirk pushed up one corner of his lips. It had saved him the effort of courting the Bartels.

"You're gonna want to see this," Conner broke into Ellis's thoughts.

Ellis motioned to the chair next to him and tossed back the last of the dark liquid lingering in his tumbler.

Conner was Ellis's brother. The middle of the three sons, he was the wise one, the one called upon for any type of knowledge. If he didn't know the answer, he knew how to find it. With computers as his partner, cyberspace allowed no one to hide.

Conner thumbed open his jacket and settled in before handing over a folder.

Ellis flipped it open. Nothing unusual. Land history. Mr. Bartel's status and all notable assets.

"You'll be most interested in the two final pages."

Ellis scanned each sheet thoroughly before pausing on the next to last. His chest tightened. "Are you sure about this?"

Conner gave a nod.

"What's Lucian D'Angelo have to do with Bartel?"

"It's all there, but my guess is he's aiming at your target."

"Who am I eliminating?" Alex strolled past him to prop a hip on the balcony railing.

"No one." Ellis kept his focus on the papers in hand as he acknowledged his youngest brother's arrival. "Yet." He flipped to the last page. "Why are you here?" he asked, keeping his eyes on the file.

"Heard you were researching."

"Can't imagine where that would have come from." Ellis shot a piercing look toward Conner.

"Admit it." Alex leaned his folded arms on his thigh that he had lifted to rest atop the railing. "I saw that glint of elation when I walked in. You miss the adventures of our working together."

"I miss the solitude of my home that went to hell when you two walked in."

"So, what are we doing?" Alex continued, ignoring Ellis's comment.

"*We* are doing nothing. I am familiarizing myself with Bartel's situation before my meeting with him." Ellis glanced at his watch. "In exactly thirty-four minutes. He gave each of his brothers a pointed look. "Alone."

Ellis couldn't miss the gleam enter Alex's eyes and realized at that moment that he would indeed not be alone. He dropped the folder onto the metal table next to the empty whiskey tumbler and pushed to his feet. "I trust the two of you will be gone by the time I return home."

Alex gave him a mock salute, and Conner simply nodded.

He rolled down his sleeves, buttoned them, and then retrieved the folder. "I have a call to make before I leave."

***

Ellis and Jackson Bartel sat across from one another in one of the finer restaurants in town. Not the most expensive. And not because Ellis realized Mr. Bartel was unable to afford a high pill. That was not a concern since Ellis was footing the bill. Expensive meals didn't always guarantee the quality to match the price. He enjoyed the atmosphere here, the service was spot on, and the food was superb. Plus, they respected his desire for privacy when he dined here. The men chatted as old friends about the weather and community events until their meals were finished and their dishes cleared.

Ellis crossed his arms on the edge of the black tablecloth. "I'm intrigued to know how I could possibly be of help to you."

Ellis focused on the transformation settling over the man facing him. He was somewhat sure what the request would be, and he was positive he was his neighbor's last resort.

Mr. Bartel pushed out a breath and looked Ellis square in the eyes when he told him. "I'm about to lose my farm."

"How does this involve me?"

"That farm has sustained my family for decades. You know I've been a proud contributor to this community. I've supplied fresh eggs and vegetables to the local grocers and straight to the people. You remember how much hay I produce. Many people depend on that to tide over livestock. At times, it keeps the smaller pets warm. Plus, I've always had extra to donate to churches and the community fall festival. And well, times have become tough what with financial strains along with the extreme weather attacking the crops. The bank refuses to extend my loan or work new arrangements. I've considered a second mortgage." The man shook his head. "But that was also a dead end."

Silence settled over the table as the waitress approached and slid a dessert dish in front of each man.

"Tough times bring tough decisions," Ellis commented as he sliced his fork through the rich chocolate cake. "What is your request?"

"I'm offering to sell you a portion of the land. We share a property line, so I hoped we could work out a deal."

Ellis sliced another bite and slowly pulled it from his fork as if he were considering the offer. Only he wasn't. He knew what he wanted and the only terms he would agree to. But it was better to let the man believe he had a bit of control over the situation, even if he didn't. At least in this situation.

"I have no need for the acreage."

"This land has been in our family, as I said, for decades. I have no sons to pass it along to who can carry on the tradition, but I would like to have a comfortable amount to leave my daughter one day. If you're not interested in the land, maybe it's possible to come to terms on a loan. I've heard tales of your providing loans."

Ellis placed his fork across the empty saucer and patted the napkin across his lips before placing it alongside the fork. "You really should try the cake. It's delicious."

Mr. Bartel's shoulders fell a bit as he raised his fork to the chocolate dessert.

"I'm sure you came prepared with numbers," Ellis surmised.

Mr. Bartel dropped his fork and straightened. Fumbling in his pocket, he pulled out a wrinkled sheet folded in quarters. "Nothing fancy. Just basic numbers."

Ellis accepted and unfolded the sheet. He scanned the numbers as Mr. Bartel finished his chocolate cake, mentally comparing them to the ones in his memory. Mr. Bartel's calculations and Conner's calculations matched. Not that he doubted they would. Conner was always spot on. And as far as his experience with Mr. Bartel, he knew him to be honest.

Ellis gave a slow nod. "We can come to terms for a loan."

"I must be honest up front that I can't afford another large payment."

"Here's what I can do . . ."

"I'm listening."

"I will clear your existing loan and hire two farmhands who will do anything you require until the end of summer. At which time we can sit down again to re-evaluate the number of hands needed to continue. Possibly any changes or updates needed to the running of things."

Bartel stared, and a long moment passed before he spoke. "My daddy taught me that if something sounds too good to be true to run. This falls into that category. What's the points here?"

"I don't want your money or your land."

Bartel's eyes narrowed onto Ellis. "What do you want?"

"Your daughter."

Mr. Bartel's eyes grew wide, and his hand ran through his graying hair, combing it back. "My daughter?"

"I take care of your problem and bring your daughter home with me."

"You want to hold my girl hostage until I repay you?"

"No repayment. Consider it a bride price."

"Absolutely not!" Mr. Bartel shot to his feet.

"Sit down." The words rolled from Ellis in a deep, low tone that all but vibrated through him.

"I know what that means. I'm not some uneducated fool you're dealing with."

Ellis remained calm as Bartel took one step toward the door and came to an abrupt stop. His brothers. Ellis never doubted they'd follow him, not even the moment he told them he was coming here alone.

Ellis cut his eyes toward the reflection in the window to confirm that fact. He threw up a hand, stopping them from approaching further, and his eyes darted back toward Bartel. "Sit down, Mr. Bartel."

"I will not sell my daughter."

"Sit down and let me explain what will happen if you don't agree to this."

Mr. Bartel's jaw tightened, his nostrils flaring. He shot another glance toward Conner and Alex standing behind Ellis. His fingers curled into fists as he eased back into his seat.

Ellis lifted a finger, summoning the waitress. "Mr. Bartel needs a Long Island iced tea."

"I need nothing from you," Mr. Bartel growled.

"Oh, but you do. Nurse that drink and hear what I tell you."

Jewelz Baxter

Chapter 2

Arabella plucked the final egg from the nest and placed it into the basket with the others. Taking her time and searching out each individual hen as if she was committing them to memory, she paused at the gate. On a sigh, she stepped through and spun with the gate as she pushed it closed. A nudge with her hip and a wiggle of the latch, it fell into place.

Smiling, she pulled in a deep breath and her eyelids drifted closed. This was her favorite time of day. The sun was dipping toward the land and the animals were settling in after a full and active day. She breathed out slowly and cast one last look around the pasture.

There standing at the fence was Burger King. His head stretched past the fence, poised for their daily chat together.

Arabella walked toward the fence and put the basket onto the ground. She reached up, stroking the animal's neck. "Good evening. Today has been quite eventful." She laughed. "I'm not sure yours has, though. Anyway, today, Papa told me he discovered a way to keep the farm. And just like you, this is the only real home I've known. Even when I moved away for college and work, neither felt like home and I looked forward to my visits back here. I really don't want to lose it."

Arabella quieted and stroked the thick gray hide, giving generous ear scratches and petting. She pulled a bag of marshmallows from the basket and dumped some into her hand, lifting it toward the bull's mouth. It took no time for the sweet and sticky treat to disappear.

"I'm going to miss you the most. I must go away for a little while. Papa didn't say how long, and I'm not quite sure I understand why or what's expected of me, but I'll be nearby. Best I gather from Papa's strange snippets of explanation is that I'll be helping out a household nearby." She glanced across the vast open field. The roof of the neighboring home popped through the bare treetops. "I hope he hasn't agreed for me to go somewhere like that. I prefer a downhome place, relaxed and appreciative."

She swiped her hand down her leg, leaving the slimy combination of marshmallow and cow slobber behind. She wrapped both arms around Burger King's neck and smiled when the animal leaned into her. "I'll see you soon, hopefully."

She leaned in once more, then stepped back and grabbed the egg basket as she swung toward the house.

***

When Arabella reached the yard, her steps slowed. A pearl white Bentley sat next to the farm truck. Her heart skipped a beat. That vehicle was no reflection of the type of family she had wanted to work for. How did anyone in this community afford such a thing? Was she going somewhere far away? Was she to leave now? She'd packed the moment she learned of the job. That only meant her possessions were ready, but she was not. She picked up her pace, rushing inside through the kitchen door. Voices drifted from the living room. Jerking to a stop, she tilted an ear toward them. She knew that voice. Butterflies appeared in her stomach and her teeth caught her bottom lip. She eased the egg basket onto the counter and turned toward the living room. Blowing out a breath, she stiffened her spine and walked through the door.

"There she is," Mr. Bartel announced and pushed to his feet.

Arabella's gaze shot to the man standing next to her father. His eyes were on her also, but he remained silent. He stood tall and confident as always, his demeanor revealing nothing. His neatly trimmed beard confessed to wisdom from experience of years more than she had lived, and his eyes were a piercing slate blue that told nothing of his emotions. Just as his smile remained hidden, she wondered what his eyes hid.

His suit was impeccable. She brushed at her shirt, hoping to remove any telltale signs of her heartfelt talk with her four-legged confidante. She glanced down. His tie must have cost more than her entire outfit. She'd seen him often and had many conversations with him. If you called them conversations—they were more like annoyances. But somehow, standing in her own home, he looked different. He presented a different perspective.

"Mr. Darby is here to pick you up."

She pushed her hair away from her face. "I must look a mess. I guess I let the time get away from me." She turned toward her father. "I gathered the eggs. They're on the counter. And don't forget Burger King's treats. He loves his marshmallows."

His smile wavered, and she knew he was attempting to encourage her. "I'll manage just fine."

"I'll go get ready."

She turned and hurried up the stairs and to her room. She paused only a moment, letting the tension drain from her body. "This is for the best," she reminded herself and moved to her mirror. She did look a mess. She was pale. Her hair was windblown, even though it had been twisted on top of her head, and wisps hung from all angles of the messy bun. She pushed her fingers through the fly-aways, hoping to add a bit of control.

"You're perfect as you are."

The deep voice brought her abruptly around to discover Ellis Darby standing in her doorway. She knew she was staring. And she wanted to argue. She wanted to tell him to leave, that she wanted nothing to do with him, just as she would have if they were standing face to face only separated by a tightly bound barbed wire. But nothing came out when her lips parted. Pushing down a swallow, she finally managed to speak. "I should say thank you for driving me. Papa didn't tell me someone would be coming, especially not you. But I shouldn't be surprised. For some ungodly reason, he trusts you."

She studied him as his eyes roamed over her childhood room. It had changed slightly along with each phase of her life.

"I regret to say the room I have prepared for you is nothing as personal as this. This reflects you perfectly."

He stepped forward, gliding his finger along the metal framework of her bed. "Antique, I imagine. Your first big girl bed. At the time, you hated it, but what little girl wouldn't prefer a new and exciting bed covered in pink and white ruffles. So, your mother worked tirelessly dressing it up with pink gingham ruffles around the bottom to match the chair cover. Along with pillows."

Arabella's gaze darted from item to item as he spoke.

"Then you grew to understand the value of the heirloom. Not the monetary value, that doesn't appeal to you, but the sentimental value did. Which is what demanded the gingham to remain all these years and after your mother passed on."

Ellis looked up to a board filled with photos, turning his back toward her. "You hold on to what's dear. You're loyal and trusting." He touched an aged photo of her with her parents, then turned back and placed a hand on each of her two suitcases. "I'll get a designer to decorate your room however you wish." He lifted her patchwork quilt from the foot of her bed and draped it over his arm, then lifted a bag. "Take your time. And don't be hesitant to bring anything of sentimental value."

He said nothing more as he stepped through the door, both suitcases in tow. How could he have known any of that? How long was he planning on her staying? She lifted the small bag from her bed that he hadn't taken and walked to the door. One last glance around and she flipped off the switch. She turned to leave but stopped. A quick spin back and she ran to the pink and white checkered chair that filled the corner of her room and jerked the pillow from the seat. She tucked it under her arm and hurried down the stairs.

Her father stood at the foot of the stairs, holding a round, wooden cheese box that had seen better days. "I put this together for you."

She took the gift, only to be relieved of everything else she held when Mr. Darby reentered the house. He turned and disappeared again without a word.

Arabella fell into her father's arms, soaking in the love for strength. "I'll be fine, Papa." She hoped she wasn't lying. She was nervous, but she was willing to do what was needed to keep the farm in the family. It would kill her papa to lose what he had worked his entire life for.

"We should go." Mr. Darby's voice cut through the sentimental goodbye.

***

The short drive to the Darby estate was made in silence. The low buzz of classical music and the darkening landscape rolling past her window reflected the thumping of her heart. Even though she had blindly agreed to this, anxiety was rearing its head, knotting her insides.

He turned into the winding drive framed by ornamental landscaping. She believed he owned as many acres as her father did, the only difference being his land was bountiful with hundred-year-old trees spreading wide and reaching toward the sky, while on her family's land, bounty was measured in crops waist-high that were plowed under yearly. Each had loyal family residing on inherited land.

Then she got a glimpse of the house. She had seen it before from a distance but never this close. It appeared to be a mansion. Strategically placed lights illuminated the cream-colored stones, making it appear bright against its dark green surroundings. With the turret corners giving it an even more regal appeal, she thought it resembled a castle in a fairytale.

Only this was no castle, and the man next to her was no prince.

Lost in her thoughts, she was still staring at the massive structure when Mr. Darby opened her car door. Her gaze dropped to his hand. Slowly, she reached out, placing her palm in his as she stood and walked with him up the steps and to the door. He tapped out a rhythm on the keypad and led her inside. "Make yourself at home. Look around. I'll be a moment retrieving your bags."

She glanced back, but he was already gone. This side of the entryway was just as breathtaking as it was from the other set against the outer stonework. Rich, dark walnut with intricately carved designs showcased three thick panes of frosted glass. A slow spin revealed to Arabella the foyer wrapped with a circling staircase which connected a balcony. A classic feel of wealth and tradition radiated from the sublime essence of the home.

The entrance door clicked, and she rushed to pull it open.

He maneuvered through the opening with all her belongings in his grip and sat them down onto the tile floor. "Let me show you around."

"Where is everyone, Mr. Darby?"

"Now, you know Mr. Darby is dead. I'm Ellis. And as for the occupants, you're looking at him."

"You live here all alone?"

"Until now." His palm pressed the small of her back and was warm and oddly comforting. "Let's get a peek at your new home."

"My new home? You make it sound as if you're never letting me go."

"You may explore more in-depth tomorrow. For now, you'll get a feel for the place." He guided her to her right. "This wing will be the most comfortable for you, I imagine. Great room. Through there is a leisure room. Half-bath farther back, and a sunroom." He redirected their path. "This side of the main floor hosts the kitchen and two dining rooms. They're all interconnected for ease of entertaining. And through the kitchen, you'll find utility rooms, including laundry and another half-bath."

He held out his palm. Hesitantly, she placed her hand in it once more, and he led her up the classic staircase where they came to a stop at the top and turned to view two separate hallways. "This direction are rooms my brothers use at their discretion." He pointed out one direction, then the other. "The door to the far end of this corridor is my office. The door before it is a game room. And here," he spun her and pushed open the door they stood next to, "will be yours."

She stepped inside. It was larger than her own room back home and appeared to be comfortable although dull for her taste with only an earth tone theme.

"We can bring in someone tomorrow to decorate it to your liking."

He gestured toward each door in the room. "Balcony. Powder room."

"And those?"

Ellis moved to grip the handles of the double doors that covered a third of the wall and pushed them open. Arabella's chin dropped. "And who's bed is that?" she blurted as if she had no idea. But she had an idea, and one she didn't like.

"I added a lock to the doors for your peace of mind."

Peace of mind? She scoffed inside. Her mind whirled and her breathing quickened. None of this felt like a situation she wanted to be in. In the house of a man she wanted nothing to do with, and to top it off, they practically shared a room. She turned what she hoped was an unnerving glare toward him. How could he stand there so calm and smug like this was normal? "I'm not sure I trust you."

"Keep them locked and you're safe. All unlocked doors are fair game." His words were firm and distinctive, giving her more reason to question the circumstances.

"Get settled in and get some rest. Tomorrow, you can wander around. Like I said, you're home now. I'll bring your things up."

She was still gaping at the room connected to hers when he disappeared. She jerked forward and grasped the door handles, slamming the doors closed. With a hard flick of the lock, she jumped back as if the touch of the metal handle would burn her.

She turned toward the other doors. First, she tried the bathroom door. It opened into a room as large as her old bedroom. The oval tub was big enough for two and sat on a pedestal. Across from the lavish place to soak, a lavatory stretched the length of the mirror-covered wall. She eased past the tub toward an illuminated alcove. A shower. But not just any shower. She stepped to the center and spun slowly. The ceiling was covered with spouts and the walls hosted jets similar to the one tucked into a high corner. She imagined it would feel like a rainstorm with water shooting from each direction.

She backed out and glanced to the door opposite the one she had entered through. No doubt it led to his room.

She twisted the knob and inched the door open. The moment her guess was confirmed, she pushed it closed and returned to her room. The door locked from the inside. She whirled, pressing her back against the door and searched the room for answers. A chair. She scurried across the room and drug the big chair to cover the door.

Stepping to the balcony door, she checked the deadbolt, assuring it was secure, and spun back toward the room. The room was sparse but comfortable. She tilted her head. Other than a landscape transformed to a sepia canvas, the walls were bare. A floor lamp now stood alone in the corner where she had pulled the chair from. A smile tugged at her lips. A perfect reading spot. A bureau and a small table blended into the ambiance of the room. The bed was narrow and appeared almost out of place with its ruffled pillow and matching white coverings. She hadn't heard Ellis step into her room, but her baggage now sat next to the wall across from her.

Ellis was nowhere in sight. She closed and locked her door and settled in for the night.

Jewelz Baxter

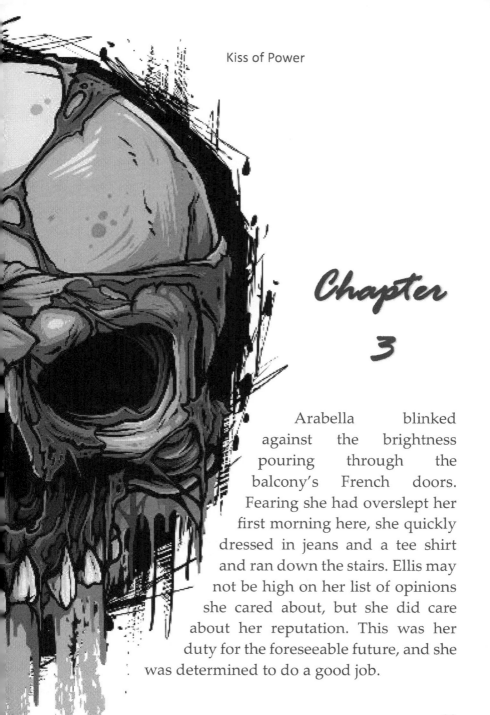

Chapter 3

Arabella blinked against the brightness pouring through the balcony's French doors. Fearing she had overslept her first morning here, she quickly dressed in jeans and a tee shirt and ran down the stairs. Ellis may not be high on her list of opinions she cared about, but she did care about her reputation. This was her duty for the foreseeable future, and she was determined to do a good job.

Silence seemed to echo throughout the massive open space as she stepped from the bottom stair. Arriving in the kitchen, she discovered a note stuck to the refrigerator door.

Meetings all morning.
Doors are locked.
Security is on.
Do not leave the house!

She plucked it from the appliance and pulled open the door. There on the shelf in front of her was another note.

Breakfast. Enjoy.

Arabella smiled and lifted the note, curious what her meal would be. It appeared to be some sort of breakfast roll.

As her food was heating, she strolled around the room, taking note of everything. Drawn to the large bay window showcasing the veranda and pool area, she became lost in the view. The microwave dinged, calling her back to things at hand, and she settled in at the long kitchen island, surprised at how delicious the simple meal tasted. Once finished, she quickly cleaned up the small mess and set out to get better acquainted with the house and see what needed to be done. Although the house appeared to be immaculate, she was one to keep on top of things.

The kitchen, she had already examined. The state-of-the-art appliances, commercial-sized oven, and efficient layout were impressive. An ideal kitchen for entertaining, just as he had said. She moved on to the formal dining room. Simple earth tones complemented the elegance of the design. Strategically placed etched mirrors elongated the feel of the space and lightened the deep brown drapes that framed tall arched windows. She glanced up and flipped the light switch. Above her, a round chandelier enhanced the taupe leather of the surrounding chairs as the metal scrolling of the fixture cast shadows onto the walls in lovely designs. Flipping the switch again, the room fell dark, and she moved on.

A smaller, yet just as elegant, dinner table filled the space next to the staircase. The two armchairs appeared comfortable and almost out of place with full sides as one would find in a living room. Their tiny floral designs brought a smile to Arabella. Even though the design was so small she had to look closely, she imagined it may be one of few, if any other, softer designed items to be found here. But she loved the look and had to agree with the designer that it perfectly complimented the six cloth-upholstered seats of macadamia brown that lined the sides.

She made her way then into the great room, pausing at the entrance to scan the wide space. It surpassed its name—it was spectacular. She roamed the area, noticing the antiques that she wondered whether they were family heirlooms or found treasures. Then there were modern sculptures and conveniences that seemed to blend well with the old. Being an interior designer herself, she pinpointed certain particulars she guessed most wouldn't notice.

The leisure room was also a delight. None of the areas of the mansion were a disappointment. Each and every one had great personality.

When Arabella moved back upstairs, she bypassed the two doors Ellis had pointed out as his brothers' rooms to use at their convenience. Which brought her back to hers. She walked in and paused at the French doors connecting his room to hers. With a twist of the lock, she swung them open and eased inside. Spinning slowly, she took in every detail. She eased onto the edge of the perfectly made bed. The space appeared to be much like Ellis—confident and mysterious. The same earth tone hues that filled the house hadn't missed this room. Mixed with black, this reflected his stately and controlled manner to the tee. She twisted, admiring the gold leaf panels reaching toward the ceiling that acted as a headboard. The sleek chandelier above her caught the sun trespassing through the glass balcony door and cast tiny rainbows about the room.

She stood and smoothed the wrinkles, removing evidence of her curiosity. The abstract art pieces that stood erect on either side of the bed caught her attention, drawing her in. They were a perfect complement to the gold leaf, with tiny swirls of gold bursting throughout the sculpted black painting. The swirls so elegant and seductive, she was unable to resist the urge to run a fingertip over one of the raised curls.

The painting wiggled and she jerked away with a gasp. That's all she needed, to break something so expensive on her first day here. She shook her head, moved to the round switch, and twisted it. The room remained dim. Her brows furrowed and she turned back toward the switch when she noticed the sliver of light kept hostage by the painting. Carefully, she eased the panel to the side and it slid open effortlessly. Relieved, she fell victim to her curiosity and walked in. "Oh, my!"

She stepped forward, running her fingertip along the sleeves of the precise arrangement of clothing. Suits. Nothing else. Each component grouped together. Shirts. Jackets. Pants. Drawers stacked waist-high stood next to rows of polished shoes. Opening the door above the drawers revealed ties, a variety but not an abundance. She closed it and moved farther into the space. A dream closet, and he used only a small portion of it. She stepped out, returned the secret door to its place, switched off the light, then walked back to her room.

Arabella pulled closed the doors and assessed her space. He had said she could redecorate. There was nothing unbecoming about the feel of the room, it just wasn't her. She did miss the challenge of decorating spaces for clients. The excitement of the hunt and the thrill of discovering that one perfect item that set a space apart or made the client giddy to display was what she loved most. But times became tough, and she saw no other option than to leave the city and move home to help rebuild the farm.

She smiled on a sigh. How long would she really be here? Would it be worth the effort? Silently, she shook her head. No need to rearrange another person's home. She'd just add a touch here and there, and when she moved out, the room would be left as if she was never here.

Arabella stepped back into the hallway and moved toward the next door past Ellis's room. The game room was massive and only partially furnished. A wet bar filled the corner for the enjoyment of drinks while playing pool. Other than the customary cue racks, the walls were bare, giving it the appearance of being neglected.

She moved on to open the last door. Intending not to snoop in his office, she leaned in, glancing to see if it may need dusting or the trash emptied. Nothing. Just as the rest of the home, it was spotless. Even the eye-catching wooden desk with its intricately carved panels appeared to be tidy. She scanned the room. His personal workspace spoke volumes to his character, as did his bedroom. Most likely, she thought, because they were the only areas of importance to him. If she had not known him and judged him from her tour, she would say he was precise, efficient, and straight forward with no tolerance of bullshit. He craved control and order.

She moved to leave but paused. Bookshelves lined the wall. It wouldn't hurt to look, she thought, so she rounded the desk. How did she miss the extra door tucked in the corner of the room? She laughed inside. A stunning desk and a wall of books, that's how. She tried the door and found a small bathroom. Smart, she thought. She closed the door and turned toward the shelves, studying the titles. Classics. A few history books. Two poetry volumes. A couple thriller crime novels. And law and criminology publications filled the shelves behind his desk.

"What are you doing in here?" Ellis's harshness startled her.

She whirled toward him, feeling her eyes stretch wide. "Looking at your library."

He folded his arms over his chest. "That explains what you're doing, not why you're in my office."

"I opened the door and was checking for trash or anything else needing to be done."

"Cleaning is not your responsibility. And if anything in here requires attention, I handle it myself. My office is off limits."

"The door was unlocked. I didn't know." She studied him, unsure whether to stay or bolt. Anger seemed to radiate from him and held her hostage. Until she noticed it, a slight drop in his shoulders.

He nodded toward the shelves nearest to him. "You may borrow any book from these shelves. These are for pleasure. Those behind the desk are work-related and I'd appreciate those not to be touched."

Arabella smiled and moved toward the books he offered, pulling out a thick novel and hugging it to her chest. "Thank you."

Ellis moved to his desk and gave a nod toward the chair facing him. "Have a seat." He perched a hip on the corner of the massive wood carved art piece.

She eased onto the edge of the nearest of the two chairs in the room and stiffened her back. With the book in her lap, her fingers curled around the edges.

"I apologize for my absence this morning, but it couldn't be avoided."

"If I'm not here to care for the house, why am I here? I can't earn my pay if I don't know what to do."

"I have a lovely cleaning lady who comes in once a week. She spends the entire day keeping the house in order. She cooks a few meals that she leaves for me to heat up when needed. I have a trusted chef who prepares larger meals when requested. The outside is handled by a reliable lawn service. So, that leaves nothing for you to fret over."

"None of that explains why I'm here."

"You, my dear, are here for me."

Arabella squeezed her eyes with a slight shake of her head before focusing back on him. "What do you mean, for you?"

"You're my companion."

"You could buy a dog."

"My counterpart then."

"You need a wife, not me."

Ellis's eyes wickedly pinned her to her seat as a corner of his mouth twitched ever so slightly.

"Oh no. You cannot kidnap me and force a marriage."

"As I recall, you came here willingly." His voice lowered to a tone that vibrated through her body. "And I don't need a piece of paper to tell me that you belong to me now."

Her stomach fluttered and, suddenly, her mouth went dry. Strained laughter echoed in her mind like a siren warning her to run. She shot to her feet. "No way. I'm going home."

"Arabella." His voice, harsher than before, stopped her in her tracks. "I'll forgive you this one time, as we haven't discussed rules nor boundaries. Sit down."

She turned, glaring at him through the narrow slits of her eyes, heat rising in her chest. She backed into the seat, her focus remaining on him. His arms were crossed now, and she could feel his eyes boring right through her.

"You sass me, you will be reprimanded. You disobey me, you will be punished. You run," his eyes narrowed more than she imagined possible, "you will regret it." Those last words rolled out so slowly and deep that her skin crawled.

"You lied."

"Not in the least."

"I'm all my father has. He would not have agreed to this." She threw up a hand in frustration. "To you holding me hostage," she clarified.

He lifted a folder from his desk and flipped it open. Sliding a sheet of paper out enough to show her the signatures across the bottom, he asked, "Is this your father's signature?"

"No," floated out on a whisper.

"I can assure you it is. I witnessed that signature. Along with mine." He returned the contract to its place and dropped the folder onto the desktop.

"I'm not marrying you, and I'm not sleeping with you," she blurted.

"Like I said, I don't need a marriage certificate. As far as sleeping, I had a bed brought in for you." He stood and moved toward the door, pausing next to her. He took her hand and tugged her to her feet. He guided her to the door just in front of him before he leaned closer. "It's not the sleeping arrangements you should be concerned with."

Jewelz Baxter

Chapter 4

A few days later, Ellis descended the stairs dressed for the day, his suit pristine, his head high and moving with purpose. It had been ingrained in him for as long as he could remember — own the best, wear the best, be the best. Even on days he never left the house, his dress was impeccable. Today would be one of those days.

His steps seemed to be a little lighter today. Even though it didn't show, he felt it. He had added another best to his list. He had chosen the best woman he could imagine. Strong, spirited, and beautiful, she complemented him perfectly. And she was in his home.

"Good morning," Mrs. Moretti, Ellis's housekeeper, greeted.

"We have a guest," Ellis announced, filling the mug that had been placed next to the coffee maker.

"I would say Alex, but he was at Conner's home two days ago. He said you kicked him out."

"I did."

"Any special requests for this guest?"

Ellis continued drinking his coffee, contemplating his answer. Arabella would buck being told what to do, but she would do it. The words nearly spilled out of him to continue her normal routine regardless of Arabella's presence. "I'll allow her to make that call. She should be down soon."

Mrs. Moretti stopped what she was doing and popped to her full height, her eyes bulging, her voice rising as she spoke. "Her? That explains why you kicked out your brother." She laughed. "Forty-seven years old and you finally found a woman to make you happy."

"I'm flattered that you believe I look forty-seven."

"Don't you realize I've worked for you long enough that I know how old you are. Granted, if you don't ease up on the stress, you'll appear sixty in no time."

Ellis wanted to argue, to tell her that he had never experienced a hard day's toil. But that would be a lie. He had never forgotten the long days of summer heat loading and unloading bales of hay. The long sleeves and gloves to keep the itching at a minimum. The salty sweat burning his eyes that his hat shaded from the sun. The weight of work boots and blisters from ropes.

He had earned every penny he made that summer. They all had, each at a different job. None of them needed the money. They were sent as spies, to gather as much information as possible to use as leverage and sabotage. Yes, those teen summers were character building in unexpected ways. That's the type of stress that had aged him—not the strenuous labor but the heartless labors.

"I know exactly how old you are." Mrs. Moretti's words cut into his thoughts. "And the fact that Conner is a year younger, almost to the day. And Alex waited two years, again almost to the day after that, to make an appearance."

A corner of Ellis's mouth lifted. "That's why I keep you around. You know too much."

She brushed off the comment with a flick of her wrist. "You keep me around because you'd be lost without me."

"Hello."

Ellis turned to see Arabella standing in the doorway.

"Hello, dear," Mrs. Moretti greeted, drying her hands on her apron.

"Mrs. Moretti, this is Arabella Bartel. Arabella, Mrs. Moretti."

Mrs. Moretti hurried around the island and pulled Arabella into a hug. "It's so good to meet you, dear. Come, sit down. I'll get you some breakfast, and we'll get to know one another."

Arabella tossed a confused look over Mrs. Moretti's shoulder toward Ellis. He nodded for her to follow but said nothing more as he moved with them toward the table. "Breakfast?" he asked and pulled back a chair, holding it as Arabella settled in at the small breakfast nook. Then he took the seat next to her.

Mrs. Moretti glanced up from the stove. "Of course, breakfast."

Ellis chuckled to himself, watching her scurrying around the kitchen cabinets. Never had she appeared excited to cook a meal for him. Not that she complained. She always offered and cooked extra treats, but there seemed to be an extra boost of energy moving her this morning.

Mrs. Moretti glanced toward the table. Not for Ellis, though. Straight to Arabella. "Dear, how do you prefer your eggs?"

"Scrambled is perfect."

"None for me, thank you," Ellis replied, even though he realized she wasn't asking him.

Mrs. Moretti cocked her head toward Ellis. "You have coffee," she stated matter-of-factly as if she was reminding a child that he could have nothing else.

Arabella burst into laughter immediately, biting her lips together when he rolled his head in her direction. "I like her already."

Obviously, he was not needed for this conversation. He raised his mug to his lips, unable to pull his gaze from her radiant smile.

In a few short minutes, they all three set at the table, Ellis with his arm on the table holding his mug, witnessing the two women bond.

Mrs. Moretti explained that she spent one day each week making a thorough run-through of the house, including laundry, cooking, and cleaning. "Tell me, do you have dietary needs I should know about? Laundry preferences? Any allergies?"

"No, ma'am, and I don't mind caring for my own needs while I'm here."

Mrs. Moretti straightened, shooting a heated look toward Ellis. "While she's here? What does she mean, while she's here?"

"She's not going anywhere, contrary to her attempts. And she's fully healthy and requires no special care." He returned his empty mug to the tabletop.

"That's true," Arabella cut in. "He checked my teeth and sturdiness before kidnapping me for his twisted amusement."

Mrs. Moretti's eyes widened, darting between the two of them. "Oh, I see."

Ellis stood. "Sass, Princess. I'm taking notes."

"Yes, sir." The tone in her voice belied her serious face as he stepped past.

As he passed through the door, Mrs. Moretti's whisper reached him. "I'm so glad he found you. Keep him on his toes."

Yes, he was glad he'd found her also. Arabella was his princess, the most valued possession he held. She had prestige and dignity that illuminated brighter than any grandeur this old mansion had ever seen. He anticipated bathing her in jewels along with any lavish desire she had. He gave into the twitch of his lips and headed up the stairs.

***

Later that day, Arabella sat in the leisure room with her sock feet tucked underneath her and her shoulder pressed against the back cushion of the small sofa. She closed the book she'd been reading and dropped it onto her lap. She had never had this much free time on her hands. Her head fell to the cushion, and she stared out into the sunny afternoon.

She had hesitated to unpack, especially after the confrontation with Ellis in his office. Delaying the chore wouldn't change her fate, so she threw her feet to the floor and stood. She made an agreement and refused to go back on her word. She was here for the duration to see it through.

Drudging up the stairs, Arabella sighed as she opened the door to her room and tossed the book to the center of the bed. Her bags remained by the door where Ellis had deposited them that first night. The only change was the large one now laid open where she'd dressed out of it. She removed the clothes, placing them onto the bed, and sorted as to where they would go. A small closet held most of them while the rest were left to fill the only four drawers in the room.

She zipped up the suitcase and rolled it into the closet. When she spun back, her attention fell onto the round box sitting atop the bureau. She was nearly bouncing on her toes as she approached it.

When she was young, her mother would take the few pieces of her grandmother's china from the cabinet and they would have a special tea party. As Arabella grew older, her mother continued that tradition at the most convenient times, days when she needed a pick-me-up.

Arabella lifted the box and pried off the lid, expecting to see her grandmother's teacups filled with memories. Instead, a folded sheet of paper greeted her.

Slowly, she lifted it and flipped it open, recognizing her father's handwriting.

You have given up so much in the name of this old homeplace. Your career, then your car, and still you never complained but continued forfeiting your own simple luxuries such as shopping and, finally, your personal connection to the outside world.

You've sacrificed too much for me to lose the only thing of value that I can one day give to you. Please forgive me for not being strong enough to tell you the truth that I'm sure you know by now.

Settle in and make the best of your home with Ellis, and I will handle things here.

You deserve to be pampered rather than laboring on this place.

Promise I'll see you when I can.

Papa

Arabella backed away slowly until her legs bumped into the bed and she dropped onto the edge of the mattress. The letter crinkled between her knees, where it hung in her hands.

It was true she had done those things without hesitation. The medical bills for her mother had become so high and home care for her was more than they could afford together. She sold off everything she had, including her budding business, and returned to provide a little bank and around-the-clock care for her mother. And she would do it all over again.

Nothing to do now but settle in and wait this thing out.

A tapping at the door brought her attention to Ellis.

"Everything alright? Have you changed your mind about redecorating?"

"Oh, no. Everything is great the way it is."

Ellis gave a nod. "Would you like to see the grounds?"

"Aren't you afraid I'll run?" She hoped she sounded as snappy as she normally was around him, but the letter had sucked all her energy.

Then he stepped forward, offering his hand like the gentleman his appearance deceived him to be. "If you do, I'll find you."

She had no fight left as she placed her palm in his. In silence, they walked outside and past the pool.

"It's beautiful here. I love how you left the natural wooded areas. It's like your own little world that you rule from your castle. Do you spend much time out here?"

"I take the occasional stroll." Ellis maneuvered a low hanging limb, holding it as she eased past.

Arabella took the lead on the worn path stretched out before her. "I mean other than to the fence to harass my bull and chickens." She flashed a grin over her shoulder.

"At times."

Arabella knew where she was headed before she reached the spot. The trees ahead were sparse with satsumas. The season was coming to an end. She had been harvesting the ripe fruit each morning before leaving the farm. She narrowed in on the few left as she drew closer.

She felt his presence next to her when she slowed to a stop but was hypnotized by the lack of orange fruit above her. "He must have hired help. He's not able to climb and cut them anymore."

"Not your concern anymore." Ellis moved to a lower limb and plucked a satsuma. Holding out his hand, he offered the citrus to her.

Arabella accepted the gift and twisted back toward the barn, scanning the area across the pasture.

A weight suddenly fell from her, making her lift to her toes, nearly bouncing as she stepped to the fence. In a flash, she shoved the satsuma into Ellis's chest, not caring if he caught it or not. Two fingers darted between her lips as she pushed out the loudest and shrillest whistle she could manage.

The bull lifted its head, swinging it in her direction.

"King! Come here, Burger King!"

"Is it his fate to be a burger?"

Arabella shot Ellis a 'go to hell' look and snapped her attention back to the large gray beast trotting toward her. "His registered name is Sterling King. When he was born, they joked that he would only be good enough for a burger, if he even lived. Papa said I should've named him Burger King instead of Stirling King. The nickname stuck."

"Intriguing. Tell me how he came to be your trained hound."

Arabella laughed as Burger King dropped his head over the barbed wire, giving her a nudge. She wrapped both arms around his neck for a quick hug before moving to ear scratches. "Mama loved livestock. Said it reminded her of times on her grandparents' farm when she was young. We would go to livestock shows just to walk around and see the various breeds and watch the cutting horses perform. She would say it smelled like home." She shivered. "I always thought it was nauseating.

"Anyway, Papa was talking to an acquaintance of his this one time as I sat with Mama to rest. She hadn't been sick for very long, but she became tired so easily. We listened to this man tell about a brahman he had that should have birthed days earlier and had become sickly. He had hands keeping watch over her, and we ended up driving to this man's ranch."

The bull lifted his head, and Arabella rubbed down his neck. "And there you were." Her palm glided between his eyes, down to his nose and back.

"Long story short, the mama had gotten into something foreign that made her sick. The vet said the calf wouldn't live. He was underweight, and if he nursed, the milk may have killed him since she was contaminated. Until they determined what the culprit was, he couldn't nurse. Of course, Mama offered to take it. The rancher was relieved to rid himself of the problem, so he signed all the papers, just in case it survived. We made a stop at the feed store for a bottle and supplements and brought him home with us. Mama held him in a blanket on the drive home. She declined quickly, but she enjoyed watching him feed and petting him from time to time."

"You cared for him." Ellis's words drifted into her memories.

"Yes. I also gathered the eggs that I added to his bottle supplement for protein. He took the bottle three times a day, and we walked around the pasture to build strength. A healthy brahman his age should weigh anywhere between thirteen hundred to sixteen hundred pounds." She flashed Ellis a grin. "Burger King here comes in at the top of that at fifteen hundred thirty-five pounds." She twisted back toward the bull as if she were conversating with a child. "The vet said we were wasting our time. We showed him, didn't we?" She planted a kiss just above his nose and stepped back. "Back to the barn," she ordered with a raise of her arm.

Arabella looped her thumbs through her empty belt loops, watching the sway of the sagging hide as the bull ambled away. A sigh escaped her as the realization sank in that she could walk here at any time. She still had a confidante and connection to home without breaking whatever contract they had.

She cocked her head toward Ellis, still silently standing next to her. She plucked the citrus back from his hand. "Lead on."

With a curt nod, he stepped around her and began the trek back toward his home.

Arabella broke open the satsuma and, without a word, stretched her arm past him. He accepted it with a "thank you" and they continued in silence, passing the pool again.

"What do you do?" Arabella wanted to know.

"About?"

"Your job. How do you earn money?"

"I was born."

"Right, the silver spoon and all."

"On the contrary. The proverbial silver spoon eluded the three of us. We were required to earn our inheritance by way of the most undesirable jobs you could imagine."

"Like the summers you worked at the farm?"

He hesitated, choosing his words. "Those were pleasant summers compared to others. But, yes, something like that."

"Okay then, what do you do now to earn money?"

"People come to me, you might say, to solve problems."

"A business consulting company," she guessed.

"Something like that." He stopped and turned to face her. "I have no qualms of sharing my personal life with you. We should share that honesty, but business is business, and I refuse to let you into that world."

"I can respect that, and I appreciate the honesty." She tilted her head and cut her eyes up to meet his. "I'm not lost to the fact that at times you evade my questions."

With a nod, he twisted toward the house. "I noticed the bountiful flowerbeds at the farm. If you wish to build beds, I can have places marked off for you."

Arabella jerked to a stop. "Like that!"

Ellis rounded to face her, calm as always. "You asked no question."

"But you knew what I meant."

"I know the perfect place you could garden." He turned and began walking away. "It's hidden to everyone other than the gardeners. They use it now for storage, but we can make other arrangements for them." They headed toward the house and beyond it to a vine-covered stone building nearly invisible from overgrown bushes and unkept trees.

Arabella moved past Ellis as he stopped, carefully choosing her steps as she leaned backward, evaluating the possibilities. "How cute. Or at least I can tell it used to be. What was it?"

"I remember it being here as a child, but we were forbidden to enter, so I'm not positive what it was used for." He stepped to the door. Gripping the handle, he threw his shoulder into the heavy wood panel, producing a pop before it creaked open. He eased in, quickly scanning the space before allowing her entrance.

"Why have you allowed it to be overrun?" She watched him, waiting for an answer or reaction, but he remained true to his unemotional self. Although, she swore a glimpse of something passed over his eyes before he spoke.

"I have no need for it."

Once again, no solid information. She moved about the small space. "It's unique. I love the blonde of the stone walls. They're beautiful with the exposed beams." She nudged a door near the back of the building. "A bathroom. Possible it could have been a guest house at one time." She turned from the small restroom in the rear corner to examine the half-wall dividing the rest of the building. With a grin, she sought out his eyes. "Explains why you don't need it. You would need friends to have guests."

"I'll notify them to clear the overgrowth."

Arabella laughed when he gave no real response and turned her excitement to gardening. "Flowerbeds along the front would set it off perfectly." She moved back outside, examining the area until the door slammed behind her.

"Decide what you need, and I'll inform the gardeners to gather it for you."

She glanced toward Ellis. "You're full of surprises today. What else have you been hiding?"

"This is pretty much it."

Arabella fell into step beside him, admiring the beauty of the place and silently planning what she'll do to occupy her time. Gardening, taking walks, and, of course, visiting the fence line.

Ellis twisted the knob and pushed open the door leading into the side of the garage. She knew it to be a garage from the large doors lining the front but had not been inside. Hmm. She wrinkled her nose and tilted her head, wondering why he parked by the steps rather than in here most times. Before the question slipped from her, she moved inside, surprised by the nearly full space with the white Bentley, a black SUV with tinted windows, and a covered vehicle with extra space on either side. "All these yours?"

"I guess you could say that."

"They're in your garage. Do you own them, or did you steal them?"

"This belongs to Gus, my driver. Then you've seen mine." He bent and lifted the corner of the car cover, sliding it back for a full view. "This one we discovered in a storage facility belonging to my father. There were more. I kept this one."

"Classic." Her finger glided along the chrome ridge dipping into a V on the driver's door of the '56 Ford Sunliner convertible. It reminded her of the mocha and ivory colors filling her current bedroom. "This is beautiful. Do you ever drive it?"

"I do. It still requires a bit of work, but it's drivable." He tugged the cover back over the car. "Can you drive a manual transmission?"

"A stick? I'm a farm girl. Of course, I can."

He jutted his chin toward the white car. "The Bentley is a '17, the last year they made that transmission. When time comes, you may drive that one if you like."

Arabella's breath caught. "What does that mean, when time comes?"

"I'd prefer to have the Ford fully restored first." He twisted, leaning his ass against the car. "Unless you would like something else."

"I can't drive that thing."

"You just said you know how."

"I mean . . ." She huffed, choosing her words. This man had thrown her another curve. "What if something happens to it?"

"It's just a car. As long as you're safe, the car can be replaced." He reached out, and she gave in to his tug and stepped closer, her fingers in his. "We've discussed house rules and boundaries. That also entails my spoiling you."

Arabella slapped her palm to his chest. "Stop being so damn perfect today! You're going to have me thinking you're sweet."

She collided with Ellis's chest, sucking in a gasp as his hand pressed against her back.

"Princess," his voice grew low, sending chills throughout, "I'm far from perfect. And nothing about me is sweet. I'm the things your nightmares and wet dreams are made of. You have the power to determine which you get."

Jewelz Baxter

Chapter 5

A week had passed since Arabella met the wonderful lady who takes care of the house. Today was her day to return, and Arabella looked forward to having someone else to talk to. After breakfast, she'd taken a stroll along the path that Ellis had shown her to have a chat with Burger King. This had not been an everyday event, but following a week of only her and Ellis in the house, Arabella was longing for communication, since Ellis was few on words. Correction, Ellis had plenty to say when he deemed fit. Casual small talk and things that interested her were not high on his list of necessary conversations. They were so different from each other that at times she wondered if they would ever find common ground.

Arabella began her slow ascension to the upper floor. Reaching the top, she twisted to see Ellis's office door open, telling her that he was settled behind that big desk of his, deep in work. Not that she understood what he did, but he would be in his office for a few hours and then leave for meetings. Some days, those meetings had lasted all day, others only an hour or two. And he never spoke when he returned. Normally, he retreated back into his office again for a few minutes. Once, he immediately disappeared into his bedroom to reemerge later showered and changed.

No matter how unconventional his work schedule seemed to her, he demanded that his business dealings were of no concern to her. That was fine with her, she wouldn't be here long enough to care anyway.

Her gaze then shot to the game room. That door was also open, which was rare. She walked to the door to find Mrs. Moretti wrapping the cord around the back of the vacuum. "Good morning."

Mrs. Moretti whirled toward her. "Morning, dear. How was your stroll?"

Arabella laughed. "How did you know I took a walk?"

"Mr. Darby informed me of your pet bull and how you like to visit him."

Ellis. Of course, he knew where she had gone. He always knew where she was. It was like she had GPS tracking built into her with a camera that he had notifications set up for. She shook those accusations away and stepped into the room. "He's a beautiful steel gray Brahman. I've had him since birth."

"Sounds lovely."

Arabella smiled and moved toward the basket of cleaning goods on the corner pocket of the pool table. "Has Ellis ever had a pet here?" She lifted a dusting wand from the cleaning tools.

"Not since I've worked for him." Mrs. Moretti straightened. "Oh, my dear," she scurried around the table and slipped the duster from Arabella's hand, "you are not to lift a finger."

Arabella's shoulders fell. "I don't mind. I need something to do around here."

"You can do anything you wish. You're the mistress of the house after all."

Arabella chuckled inside. Mistress of the house. "I'm not even sure what that means."

"I admit," Mrs. Moretti began with a shake of her head, "that may be an outdated term these days. But where I come from, it's an honor. And you very much fit the title. Embrace it without question."

"An honor to be considered responsible for something I have no control over? Not to mention none of this is mine to make decisions over."

Mrs. Moretti sent her a supportive look and then returned to her dusting. "You'll figure it out."

Arabella eased around the room. "For a game room, this one is sparce of any character. Or entertainment options." She spun, taking in the massive size. "Did it used to be something else? It's twice the size of any room other than Ellis's bedroom."

"I can't say."

Arabella moved to the window and peered across the roof of the garage and through the maze of limbs and leaves. "I have yet to see a bad view from any window."

"Mr. Darby is quite particular with all aspects of the home. Even the rarely seen views."

The sun was beginning to warm the windowpane and seep into the room. Arabella could feel the summer heat threatening to arrive early. She twisted and pressed her back to the wall. "I thought that also, but he showed me a cottage on the premises that appeared to have been neglected for years."

Mrs. Moretti popped erect, and the dusting wand fell to her side.

Arabella pushed from the wall. "Are you all right?"

Mrs. Moretti turned toward Arabella. "Oh, yes." She laughed. "I'm just surprised Mr. Darby would overlook any detail."

"Do you happen to know anything about it?"

"I only care for the home. I venture nowhere else," Mrs. Moretti stated flatly.

"Oh, I didn't mean—"

"I know what you meant, dear. And there is nothing I can share about such a place. But I'd love to hear about it." She moved to another spot and continued with her work.

Visions of stately rose bushes framing the massive door and bursts of color adorning the window boxes popped into Arabella's mind. Her tongue darted across her bottom lip as she mentally jotted to-do notes.

"Is it a horrendous place?"

Arabella sucked in a breath at the reminder she was not alone. "Not at all. It does need a bit of cleaning and a little love, but overall, the place is wonderful. It reminds me of a cottage one might see in brochures of Europe. Bleached stone walls with a gorgeous arch separating the two sections of the building. And the roof reminds me of those . . . what do you call them? Like clay pots broken in half and lined on the rooftop?"

"Terracotta? A clay roof?" Mrs. Moretti offered.

"That's it!"

"Like a Tuscan-style country home?"

Arabella grinned. "Exactly. Or at least what I recall from photos."

"What did Mr. Darby tell you about the place?" Mrs. Moretti asked, not missing a beat of carrying out her chore.

"Not much. He didn't know any of its history, just that it had been there for as long as he could remember." Arabella's shoulders squished toward her body, as excitement of the project bubbled up inside. "He offered to clean it up and allow me to landscape it. Roses and maybe something colorful for the windows. And to the side, a small vegetable garden."

"Lovely idea. I hope to see this project when it's completed."

Arabella dropped onto the arm of a chair near the corner opposite the pool table. Her shoulders deflated, the thrill of the task gone. "I'd love to do the gardening. But then I wonder if it's worth it. Will he keep it up after I'm gone? And an endeavor that size could take weeks. What if I don't finish?"

Mrs. Moretti replaced the dusting tool back into its place in the basket. "First of all, any project that you enjoy doing is not a waste of time, no matter the circumstances. Secondly, why would you think that you would be leaving here? Aren't you happy?"

Arabella pushed out a breath. "I'm not sure what to think. Ellis brought me here on false pretenses, I'm afraid. But neither he nor my father are willing to elaborate on the issue. That leads me to wonder the true reason for my stay and the length of it."

Mrs. Moretti cocked her head and wrinkled her forehead.

The confusion on the woman's face stung, bringing her to blurt out her assumptions. "I'm collateral for a loan. Okay? I hate to admit that, but I'm here out of necessity, not because either of us want me here."

Mrs. Moretti's lips twitched before she straightened and searched out Arabella's eyes. "Seems to me Mr. Darby has never brought *collateral* into his home. Nor does he allow anyone on the premises he doesn't want here, let alone into his home." She lifted the basket. "You're a young and vibrant woman who appears to be intelligent. I can't imagine you allowing anyone to control your life. You could walk out at any time and discover a way to repay the so-called loan." She paused with a smile. "So, why are you really here?"

Arabella's chin dropped. She couldn't tear her eyes from the woman walking out of the room. She fell into the cushioned seat and leaned her head against the side of the high back that curved forward. Why was she here? She could return to Dallas to any time and step back into the design industry. Or other places, it didn't need to be Dallas. She could adapt to any city and make a living. So, why did she remain in a place that gave her no financial stability or chance of growth? Her entire body fell lax. Because gratification wasn't measured only in job titles or money.

She pulled in the fresh lemony scent filling the room and pushed to her feet. Tugging the hem of her shirt smooth, she rolled her shoulders and walked from the room. A glance down the hallway confirmed Ellis remained in his office. The walkway seemed to lengthen as she made her way toward his open door.

The threshold was her limit. She raised her hand, but before her knuckles announced her presence, he abandoned the papers he'd been intently studying and looked her way. "Yes?"

"I was just wondering if there was anything I could do for you?"

Ellis's brow twitched. "That's a loaded offer."

She lifted her chin. That may not have sounded as she intended. "Would you like a drink, or is there something around the house I can help with?"

"I prefer your original offer." He leaned back in his chair, causing it to tilt backward. "But we could have a drink and do things around the house."

She closed her eyes, containing the shiver threatening her body. This is why she didn't talk to him often. Her gaze lifted back to him, and she tucked her hands into her jean pockets. "I could prepare some lunch if you're hungry."

"Mrs. Moretti has lunch taken care of." He cocked his head." But I'm open for dessert."

Arabella's lips parted but nothing came. She should just retreat and walk away.

"Is there something I can do for you, Miss Bartel?"

His lips twisted into a lopsided smirk, and his eyes glimmered with a wickedness she had witnessed there before. Definitely time to retreat. "No, I'm good," spilled from her and she whirled away, giving him no time to rebut.

***

Later that same evening after dinner, Arabella and Ellis retired to the great room for a nightcap. She studied him for a moment as he savored the last of his drink and returned the tumbler to the small table next to him. "You're not exactly what I imagined. Not far off, but you're bearable to live with. I'm willing to call a truce for the time being. Don't get me wrong, I'm still unhappy with being drug here."

"So, you no longer claim kidnapping? You are indeed warming up to me."

"I believe you lured me here to torture me for your amusement."

"Lured, I can admit to. Torture? What type of sweet torture do you desire?"

A nervous laugh escaped her. "What? Do you have a basement you plan to toss me into?"

"Regretfully, no dungeon basement. But we can transform that little shack on the grounds if you so like. Or, we do have an entire mansion to explore a multitude of possibilities. Which brings up the likelihood of a safe word."

"Safe word?"

"A prearranged word or signal."

"I know what a safe word is. What I don't know is why you think I would need one."

"To unambiguously indicate you've reached your limit. That limit may be emotional, physical, or moral. A situation may arise and you may find yourself in danger or in need of help. That signal informs me of the severity of the situation. Contrary to belief, they are not just for sexual play."

She stared for a long moment. "So, you're saying if I get into trouble, this will help you rescue me? Or if you're irritating me, I just call out this completely random word we agree upon, and you'll leave me alone? Like I yell 'Penguin Master' and you'll back off and leave?"

Ellis's jaw clenched, holding back his grin. She was baiting him, and he found it amusing. He stood and motioned for her to follow. Stopping at the bottom stair, she turned, standing eye-level with him.

"Princess, you may well call me 'master'," he leaned closer, "but for the safe word, how about we use eagle? Because I'll protect you as fierce as one, but I'll also swoop in and take you, like the eagle scoops up his prey." His beard brushed her cheek as he straightened and stepped around her, leaving her rooted to that spot.

Jewelz Baxter

Chapter 6

Ellis stood on the balcony looking down toward the pool. The rippling water gave the blue and green bottom a distorted look. As he stood watching, blinding rays bounced from the water sporadically as if the sun played peekaboo behind the clouds that chased each other across the sky.

But the pool was not what he found interesting. He had caught sight of Arabella lounging next to it and he was unable to walk away. Her bare feet were cooling in the water as she sat on the side. Rain had filled most of the night before and the air had turned into a muggy heat. She had pulled on a pair of cutoff jeans and a top that hung from her shoulders by thin straps. He imagined it was the skimpiest thing she owned, and there was no way she donned a bra underneath that thing, which he felt was no larger than a handkerchief.

As time went by, she swung her feet to the concrete and leaned back, tilting her face toward the sun for the few seconds it had chosen to show itself. The instant another cloud pushed away the brightness, her eyes popped open, landing on him.

Ellis leaned his arms onto the rail as if he had just walked up. He was never at a loss for words, and even though he remained silent now, words bombarded his brain. Only none of them he thought were appropriate to yell across the way. No, these thoughts he wanted to plant in her ear closely and intimately. When he moved her into his home, he vowed to himself to make her feel comfortable and relaxed before staking his claim. His gaze took her in, from the twisted hair pinned to the top of her head to her bare orange toes. Orange. He cringed inside. That would need to change. More importantly, how more relaxed could she get? Yes, she was ready.

"Join me?" Her words lifted toward him, cutting into his evaluations.

He turned and dropped his suit coat from his shoulders, tossing it onto the bed as he passed. Hopping down the stairs two at a time, he unbuttoned and rolled up his sleeves. He preferred to remain in the comfort of the air conditioning, but duty called, and he hoped the adjustments would aid in withstanding the heat. He stepped through the door, greeted by her lovely smile.

He dropped onto the edge of a lounge chair and leaned forward, resting his forearms on his knees. "You should be swimming."

"Have you ever swam in it?"

"I've made laps a few times."

"Of course, you swim laps. You sound as if having fun is beneath you." She hopped to her feet and made her way to stand inches away from him. He straightened and looked up, studying the concentration on her face as her fingers fumbled near his neck. She reached for his tie. "It's a hundred and ten out here and you're dressed for the office." She slipped the tie from him and looped it around her own neck. "Chill a bit and relax."

Her fingers burned straight through the fabric of his shirt as she worked each button until she deemed it to be open enough. "There! Isn't that better?"

He followed her movements. From the balcony, he guessed at the thin material she trusted to hide her body. From this distance, he realized it was indeed teasingly thin. It molded to her curves like a second skin when she stretched out in the lounge chair next to his. Perfect mounds rose and fell when she breathed deep, one nipple pushing hard to be uncovered. Damn. If it was this erect relaxed, what would it do under his manipulations? His tie lay across her other breast, hiding that pebble.

He twisted and stretched out his legs, crossing his ankles.

"I love the clean air after a rain," Arabella said, taking another deep breath.

"Only the devil himself would bask in this heat," Alex laughed as he appeared at the door, bringing Ellis's plans to an abrupt halt. "And here you are."

"Why are you here?" Ellis squinted against the sun as his brother pulled a chair next to him.

"Howdy, ma'am."

Ellis rolled his head toward Arabella. She lifted a hand with a quick wave and took another cleansing breath with no concern for the newly arrived company. He returned his focus back to his brother. Anyone else and he would have sent Arabella inside to cover herself, but other than a customary glance to say hello,

Alex wouldn't indulge in the view. That was a code none of them would ever cross with each other.

Alex ran a finger under his collar, stretching his neck. "You know, the Texas heat is bad, but I don't know any place that can rival the mugginess of Louisiana."

"Perfect reason for you to return to Texas."

"You know we're a team. You would be lost without my talent."

They were a team, each with a different set of skills. They had been taught to work together. Ellis dropped his head to the chair and closed his eyes. "I'm willing to take that chance."

"I got that house I looked at."

Ellis's heart lifted a bit. Not that he would ever admit it aloud, but they did belong in the same town. "Please tell me it's in Texas."

Alex chuckled. "It's about four miles from here."

"Oh, lucky me."

"I can't very well stay here now that you have . . . um," he cleared his throat, "a companion."

Ellis acknowledged the fact with a nod.

"I can get out of Conner's space too. And we're back together."

"Selling the lake house?"

"Hell no. It's on the lake, and it belongs to us all now. I'm transferring it into the trust."

Ellis swung his feet to the ground. "Let's take this to the office."

Alex slapped his hands together, rubbing them excitedly. "That's what I'm talking about. Straight to business." He jumped to his feet.

Ellis led him up the stairs, keeping silent until reaching the office. He rounded the desk, falling into the large, cushioned leather chair. "I thought you were keeping busy hiring out?"

Alex tilted his head side to side. "It's not bad. I can do that from anywhere."

"But you'd rather be here to get under my skin, is that it?"

"We can open a shell. All of us together again can roll in the money. Maybe a legit business. Hell, I get antsy waiting around for a job. Get Conner on the line. I'm ready to hit a home run."

Ellis clenched his jaw and reached for the phone on his desk. The three of them parted ways when their father died two years ago. He returned to the home they'd grown up in that he had inherited. Conner remained in Texas and followed a year later back to this town. Alex headed to the lake for a life of leisure. Now, here he was. The only surprise to Alex's decision was the timing. Ellis had figured Alex to have another few months of partying in him before seeking out a reunion.

Ellis dialed the number and leaned back as ringing echoed throughout the room.

"What's up?" Conner's voice replaced the shrill ringtone.

"If I must suffer, you must too."

Conner laughed. "What did Alex do now?"

"I'm gracing the two of you with my presence. You should be celebrating."

"You've been gracing me with your presence for two months now. Is Ellis getting his turn now?"

"No!" Ellis blurted before Alex could clarify his meaning.

When Alex's chuckle died, he elaborated. "I bought a house. I'll be moving here permanently."

"We're back in business," Conner announced.

"That's what I said." Excitement spilled from Alex, but he was always the one to share his emotions and work excited him. Ellis had learned early on that Alex thrived on the adrenaline of planning and executing a job.

Ellis breathed in deep, choosing his words. He had few objections to the plan, but things needed to be different this time. "Be sure this is what you each want."

The room filled with heavy silence, and Ellis studied Alex as the implications settled into his brother's thoughts.

"The old man isn't here anymore." Conner's voice came through the speaker harsher than moments before. "I'm free. When?"

Ellis's muscles tensed. He hesitated a moment before agreeing. "Tonight. Not here."

"My place. I'll shoot you each the address," Alex offered.

"Done. I'll see you there." Conner's line went silent.

Alex stood with a grin. "I'm off furniture shopping. We'll need somewhere to sit."

With a single nod, Ellis watched his brother stroll from the room. He dropped his head to the back of the chair, listening to the rain tick against the window behind him. Things seemed to be falling into place.

Minutes later, he walked from his office and down to the main floor. Arabella stood in the great room, leaning a shoulder against a windowsill.

"The rain run you back into the house?"

Arabella dropped her head onto the windowsill. "Yeah."

"Did you finish the book I saw you reading this morning?"

"I did. I'll return it to your office." She rolled her body along the wall until she faced him. "Can I go to the library?"

"The library?"

"I've read everything in the house."

"If that is what you wish to do, I'll take you."

"I'll grab some shoes and my purse." She ran past him and up the stairs.

In the few moments it took for Ellis to stroll to the entranceway and retrieve his keys, Arabella was running down the stairs toward him. She appeared almost giddy as she came to a stop next to him. "I'm ready."

He took in her well-worn boots she'd added to her cutoffs and that barely-there top. At least that hideous orange on her toes was hidden. "Prepare to spend the day tomorrow shopping."

"For what?"

"Appropriate attire."

Arabella leaned and twisted, studying her clothes. "What's wrong with this? Not bougie enough for you?"

"I've quite enjoyed it. And I'll continue to enjoy it as I follow you into the library. But the first set of eyes I see looking your way inappropriately, I assure you, I will gouge them out."

"You can't do that."

"Try me."

She threw her hands to her hips and narrowed her eyes. "You don't get to tell me what to wear, and now,

I'm not going anywhere with you. You can just kiss my ass."

"Don't threaten me with a good time."

She folded her arms and popped her hip out, cutting him a look he was sure was meant to offend.

He only narrowed his eyes with a gleam to trump hers. "When I kiss that pretty little ass, I won't stop until my lips have tasted every inch of you. Every. Delicious. Inch." The last of his words were drawn out as he closed the gap with each syllable. He paused, making sure his point was understood. "Now, get in the car, or the belt comes off."

***

He followed her in, sought out a seat that kept her in view, and settled in. The library was small, with three distinct sections—children, teens, and adult. The adult section consisted of five isles. Past the five walls of books were two cushioned chairs and a table. It was one of those seats he used as she scoured shelf after shelf.

Ellis followed her every move, watching how her denim shorts stretched across her ass when she bent over. When she leaned forward facing his direction, he knew she had no idea her shirt dipped, offering an enticing view of those ample, pink-tipped mounds.

Arabella placed another book onto the stack she'd begun piling on the floor. She picked it up and moved to the table. "I'm ready."

He said nothing as he stood and stepped behind her. He felt the jolt of her body the instant his hand touched the skin beneath her shirt, but he gave her no time to bolt. His palm pressed her stomach, bringing her flush to his chest. He loved the way she gasped when he brushed his beard across the side of her neck. When he did this before, she was at a loss to hide the sensation that it triggered. There it was again, a ripple of pleasure shooting through her, pebbling her skin under his palm. "Princess, this is why you're dressed inappropriately." He pressed the growing bulge of his pants into her hip. "But that's my dismay and your reprieve," he stepped back, "for now."

She hesitated to move and never looked at him. Finally, she turned and bolted to the checkout desk.

Ellis strolled past as she slid her library card across the counter and waited for her at the door. She nearly ran past him, avoiding eye contact as she hurried toward the car. If she thought running from him would ease his lust, how wrong she was. He strolled behind her, noticing each bounce of her body until she slammed the car door closed.

He settled into the car and adjusted his cock with a quick sideways glance toward her. Did those rosy cheeks indicate she was heated as much as he was? Most likely, he concluded. Her skin blushed brightly until it dipped under that 'come hither' top.

"Where else would you like to stop?"

"Home." Arabella blurted. "Please take me home."

'Take me' echoed in his mind. He stared ahead to the road. Yes, she would soon be begging him to take her. "Home it is. You sound flushed. Everything alright?"

"I . . . um . . ."

He kept her in the edge of his vision as she fumbled with the stack of books. She froze a moment before blowing out a breath and jerking two books from the pile.

"I got these for you." She held them up. "Oh, but don't look now. Just drive. I'll hand them to you at home. Your house. Ooh."

Ellis reached across the console without looking and slid his hand onto her leg. "Maybe you need something to help you relax."

Her muscles tightened under his touch and she let out a gasp. "Really, I'm . . . I'm fine."

His fingers drew large circles over her thigh. He shot a glance toward her. She resembled a statue clutching her books and staring through the windshield. A devious grin took over his lips and he lifted his hand back to the wheel, relieving his left hand. Propping his elbow on the door, his fingers wrapped around his beard, pulling the slight curl in it straight and recalling the goosebumps it initiated. He had always kept it short and well groomed. How would she react to it lengthened? More to tease with should ignite more shivers, something he planned to find out. "I hope you don't mind that I have to leave you at the house alone for the evening."

"No problem."

He pulled up to the house and parked at the foot of the steps. "If you wait a moment, I'll have an umbrella."

"No need." She jumped from the car and ran to the door. He jogged up the steps behind her and called out the series of numbers as she pushed the buttons. The instant the door opened, she darted inside.

Ellis moved inside, brushing the droplets from his suit as he watched her run up the stairs. Dropping his coat from his shoulders, he draped it over the hall tree and made a straight line to the wet bar. Nothing seemed appealing to him. No doubt Alex would have plenty of alcohol tonight to kill his thoughts. He knew his brother—he'd have enough to clear all three of their minds.

He checked the time and turned toward the kitchen, glancing up the staircase as he passed. Arabella was still hidden behind her closed door. No surprise, but she couldn't hide all night. He continued to the kitchen and filled an ice bucket, then on to the wine rack, where he chose one and deposited it into the ice. He stopped by the stemware and cast another glance toward the second floor as he passed through, heading to the leisure room. Ellis placed the bucket and goblet on the end table by the sofa and returned to the stairs. Reaching the top, he tapped on her door.

The door swung open. "I thought you were leaving." Ellis took in her overly baggy tee and leggings. "What's wrong with me now?" she blurted before he could speak. "I'm comfortable. Sorry it hides my butt."

"Princess, that hides everything."

"Good." She tossed her head and crossed her arms.

"I must step out for a bit. I'll drop back by before leaving for the evening."

"Thanks for the warning." She moved to close the door.

He threw his hand up, catching it. "I left a little something for you in the leisure room. I thought it'd be a nice place for you to read while I'm away." He noted the fade of her resistance at his words.

"Thank you." Her voice was low as he turned away. "Ellis?" He paused, twisting to see her. "Would you like the books?"

He gave a nod. "Just leave them by the sofa. I'll pick them up when I come in."

Arabella smiled and moved back into her room.

He headed down the stairs. Of course, he would enjoy the books, among other things.

Jewelz Baxter

Chapter 7

Ellis pulled into the driveway of the address Alex had sent. He pulled to a stop next to his brothers' cars and turned off the engine. He stared across the steering wheel toward the dark dwelling. Slowly, he stepped from the car keeping his eyes on the house and quietly pushed the door closed. A prickly sensation settled over his scalp, drowning out the chirping and light rustle of leaves around him. The sun had only begun to dip behind the rooftop, sending him into a shadowed mystery.

His hand dipped inside his jacket to rest on his gun as he focused on the surrounding sounds coming back to life. He reached the door and pushed it open. "Alex?"

He paused, waiting for the reply that didn't come. "Alex! Conner!" Gun in hand, he eased through the dimly lit house only to be met with silence.

The place was empty, each room void of any sign testifying to the ownership of the home. He lifted his arm, holding steady on the open back door, each step slow and calculated.

They had enemies. Anyone who danced on the dark side of the law learned to always be vigilant. He could not afford the luxury of taking chances.

Time seemed to slow as footsteps clapped against the concrete, drawing closer. Both arms steady, he locked a bead on the door and waited.

The door swung open, and his barrel was spot on the face of the intruder.

"Damn. If you don't like the place, just say so." Alex's eyes met his across the barrel. He paused, then walked on past, making room for Conner to enter.

Ellis relaxed and popped his weapon back into its holster. "Don't you have electricity?"

"Not yet."

He fell into step behind them and returned to the kitchen. Alex grabbed pizza boxes from the counter in passing, only stopping at an alcove across the room. Long and rectangular, it had the feel of a walk-in closet if not for the windows circling the top half of the walls.

"Here we are." Alex dropped the two pizza boxes onto the floor and settled between them. "Have a seat. Grab a beer from the chest."

Conner dropped to the floor, stretching his legs out and crossing them at his ankles. "Weren't you furniture shopping today?"

Ellis flipped open the ice chest and passed out the cans.

Alex accepted one and popped the top. "Decided this was more appropriate."

Ellis took his place on the floor opposite Conner and flipped the tab of his beer. "Regression or a therapy tactic?"

Conner jerked his head up. "You too?"

"This is the reason I decided on this place." Alex lifted a slice of pizza from a box. "I knew the two of you would appreciate it as much as I do. I'm thinking bench seats with a long slim table between them."

"The benches in the Grove," Conner recalled.

Alex gave a nod and turned toward Ellis. "Are they still there?"

"They are," Ellis confirmed.

"Ever go out there?"

Ellis bit into his pizza. He would rather avoid that subject, not of the benches but of the reason those hidden seats had become a safe place.

"Come on, man. It's us. Just like when we were kids hiding in the closet at home. You gotta let it out sometimes or those memories will haunt you forever." Alex dropped his head to the wall behind him. "I know they do me."

Conner returned his beer can to the floor. "Yeah, they do. Tying up ends and moving in different directions has done nothing to stop them."

Ellis dropped his head, staring at the slice of various toppings in his hand. "I go out there and sit when I need to. There is still no visible worn path. I take a different approach each time, just like the old days." He looked up. "And just like you need this enclosed space and Conner needs his basketball."

Conner's head bobbed slowly before dropping it back against the wall. "The only time my thoughts were clear was on the court. Then I would look up and imagine a face above the rim and slam it as hard as I could."

"Still play?" Alex asked.

"When my head takes over. I can stay out there for hours shooting hoops until I'm too exhausted to think." Conner rolled his head toward Ellis. "You appear to have your life together. You have Arabella now."

Yes, he had Arabella in his home, but nothing about his life was so-called put together. "Appearances can be deceiving."

"So, you used a little leverage to get her there. You fall in love and life is good."

"I highly doubt that's possible. My lessons on love were not love." Ellis's jaw ticked. "The screams and cries of the women that he . . ." He lifted his eyes toward his brothers, knowing the same lessons had been forced upon them. "I'm afraid to touch her."

"I get it. I've had dates tell me I needed therapy and then they disappear," Alex confessed.

"I'm sure we all do," Conner agreed.

"If we unload it to a therapist, that person will need a counsellor of their own," Ellis surmised.

Alex huffed a chuckle. "That's no shit."

"So, we stick to our tried-and-true devices." Conner raised a beer. "And be thankful we can now afford better beer and hot pizza."

That brought a raised beer from each of them along with a laugh. When they were young, their father would drag them along when he paid local store owners a visit. He would be too busy relaying a message or receiving a payment that he never realized they'd stolen a beer can each to sneak into the house. Then they would manage to have a pizza delivered to a designated place on the property, sometimes leaving money in the spot, other times they'd acquired a credit card number. One of them would sneak it to Alex's closet while the others kept watch.

After their father thought them asleep, they would hide in the closet, whispering, with warm beer and cold pizza.

Their arrangement worked for years. Until junior high, when their father discovered an empty beer can. He went into one of his rages. If they were going to drink, they would drink like men. Beer was for the common low class, he would say. A wet bar was installed in the grand room and, from that point on, was always kept well stocked with "manly" liquor their father deemed good enough to consume.

He never discovered the pizza. He never would have approved of it. Truth be told, they imagined he would have shut down the pizza shop for making the deliveries, not to mention punish the delivery drivers.

"We should open a brewery," Alex suggested.

"Now, there's an idea," Conner agreed.

"It could work," Ellis agreed. "Legit storefront would bed us into the community better. After this many years of leaving this place behind, many people still fear the name."

"No doubt the older citizens remember his reign. We take that fear and twist it to our advantage," Alex suggested.

"Does anyone ever think about our mother?" Conner changed the subject.

"Which one?" Alex asked.

"Our biological mother. Not those fake ass stepmother wannabes. Ellis, you would have the best memories."

"I was five when she left, so not much."

"I've looked for her," Conner admitted.

Ellis and Alex jerked their attention toward their brother.

"I began thinking. Not one of those women showed at father's funeral. You'd think they would have wanted to be sure that son of a bitch was dead. I couldn't locate any of them."

"Dead," Ellis surmised.

"You think our mom is dead too?" Alex asked him.

"I don't know." Conner's voice was hopeful.

"Most likely." Ellis's voice was low.

The room was doused in silence and darkness as Alex fumbled a bit before light radiated from his side. He moved the lantern to the center of the space. "So, boss, how did you get away from your lady tonight?"

Ellis rolled his head toward Alex. "Boss?"

"No need to change the order of things," Conner agreed. "This is how we work best. The Eagle, the Hawk, and the Owl. It's what we were raised to be."

Ellis gave a nod. He wasn't wrong. They had each been raised with specific skills to complement each other. "I told her I was meeting you two losers. She gets the truth."

"Better she knows the real you now," Conner advised. "Take it from me. Free the beast early on. It's worse the longer you prolong it."

Free the beast. Ellis bit into his pizza. He was more of a beast than even they realized. He had become so accustomed to hiding himself that he doubted he could let go. Which was for the best anyway. Arabella never needed to be witness to any of his scars. He dropped his head to the wall, and Conner and Alex's voices faded to a low buzz. How would she react? Could she accept his true self? His dark side? His gut laughed, mocking his desires. She had only now accepted him as human instead of a nuisance. Was he willing to cross the line and take that chance?

"Ellis!"

He jerked toward Conner. "You on board with that? I know you've established our presence. You ready to roll with it?"

"Of course, he's on board and ready. He's already calculating plans as we speak." Alex raised his beer. "To the Darby second generation."

Ellis nodded and raised his can. "All or nothing."

Jewelz Baxter

Chapter 8

Arabella's evening had been magical. A wonderful twist to end a dreary day. Ellis had gotten under her skin, which was nothing new. But then, as usual, he did something sweet. The moment she was confident she was alone, she carried the two thrillers that she'd chosen for him down to the leisure room as he had asked. There waiting for her was a thoughtful bottle of wine, one she couldn't resist. She poured a glass, curled up on the end of the sofa, and fell into her book. Somewhere around chapter four, Ellis had popped his head into the room long enough to inform her that he was only back to drop off food for her and would be heading to his brother's home for the rest of the evening. She'd thanked him for the food and returned to reading.

Sometime later, Arabella closed her book. She had no idea of the time or how long she'd been lost in the story. The ceiling-high windows were black, no stars or moon in sight. Not even a silhouette of treetops stood proof of the wall being transparent. She stood and stretched her back side to side and rolled her neck. Tucking the book under her arm, she gathered her wine goblet and the rose that Ellis had left with her delicious Mexican meal. She flipped the switch, leaving the room in total darkness, same as she did with the great room when she passed through.

She meandered up the stairs, leaving only the foyer light burning for when Ellis returned home. Stepping into her room, she sucked in a breath. Another surprise. She placed the rose and glass on the table next to her bed and lifted the beautiful robe. She held it to her body, glancing down at the deep emerald hue. Imaging the luxurious feel of the silk hugging her body, she whirled toward the bathroom.

Stuck to the mirror was another sweet gesture. She tugged the note from its spot and read.

My princess deserves pampering.
Rose petals for soaking
Wine for relaxing
Silk for pleasure

Arabella was lost to control the grin that overcame her. Lifting her eyes toward the mirror, she spotted another gift. She turned and moved to the elegant tray stretched across the tub. Deep, rich mahogany, in a perfect accent to his style, held the rose petals he'd hinted of. In a flash, she retrieved her wine, stripped, and was perched on the edge of her spa for the night, hypnotized by the rising bubbles.

Twisting the knobs to stop the flow, she stepped in and slid down with a sigh until her neck nestled against the curve of the porcelain. Her eyelids drifted closed as she inhaled the fresh floral scent. A simple luxury she hadn't realized how much she missed until this moment. Her muscles soaked up the heat until she felt no urge to move. Not even to her bed. A half-hour later, in now tepid water, she flipped the plug, sure if she didn't move now, she'd drift to sleep and awaken in ice water.

Arabella stepped out and grabbed a towel, drying as she moved to the mirror. Her gaze fell upon the note and thought of Ellis. Would he return home tonight?

He had mentioned that at times, each of his brothers slept here. Did he stay there occasionally also? She placed the towel on the vanity and slid the robe up her arms, wrapping herself in luxury. She looped the sash of her new robe into a bow, recounting her lovely and relaxing evening.

Steam from the luxurious bubble bath still lingered around the mirror like a halo while the fresh scent enveloped the room like a comforting hug. She released a clip from her hair and reached for her brush when the door burst open.

She whirled on a gasp at the sight of Ellis in the doorway. The glint filling his eyes as they traveled the length of her rendered her motionless. She worried her lip, falling into the depth of his stare as he closed the space between them. "I'll be out of your way."

"You've been on my mind."

Her mouth suddenly went dry. "Can't say the same," she pushed out, hoping it sounded sincere.

Ellis moved another inch closer. "Liar."

Her tongue slid across her lower lip.

"That tongue," he groaned.

She shoved at his chest only to have his fingers curl around her wrist, jerking her to him.

"Get out." She punched his chest until his hand became tangled in her hair.

"I told you, unlocked doors are fair game." Heat seemed to radiate from him, filling her, leaving her throat dry. Her tongue darted out again, running along her lower lip.

"Don't do that," he growled, his gaze following the path of her tongue.

"Do what?" She knew the words drifted from her, although she heard nothing over the pounding of her heart. Her tongue darted out once more, attempting to spread what little moisture was left in her mouth onto her lips.

"That." He reached, his finger trailing her tongue's path across her lip.

His grip tightened, sending pain through her scalp like fireworks. Her gasp was silenced by his lips. His tongue forced hers back into its home where they sparred, and he stifled her scream with a swallow. Her fist again pounded his neatly pressed suit. Each punch to his shoulder, he pressed her arm that he had twisted behind her back, pulling her deeper into his chest.

She forgot what she held in her hand but heard it tumble to the floor when she bumped into the lavatory. Her fingers twisted in his jacket, clenching tight.

He bucked against her, pressing his erection into her hip. His mouth abandoned hers, and she gasped for breath. The pain in her scalp eased and her head relaxed. Her fist slid down his chest, twisting in the opposite lapel, causing her fingers to whiten from their grip.

She tried to think, to maneuver an escape. It was no use. Even if she could have formed a coherent thought at that moment, the warmth of his breath on her ear sent her into a fog.

"That's right, hold tight," he coaxed.

The coolness of the floor fell away from her bare feet as her bottom collided with the lavatory. His suit coat hit the floor. Was it his hands pulling it away or hers pushing it from him? She couldn't be sure, as they were now intertwined, moving behind her and trapping her yet again. He held her firm and began his attack on her resolve, nipping at her earlobe with a slow and continuous move downward. Teasing the delicate area of her neck and shoulder, he grazed her skin with his teeth, sending chills down her spine. He bit into her robe, jerking it open. Her fight faded, replaced by a heat filling her core and rendering her helpless. Her chest rose heavily, thrusting her tightened nipple farther between his lips. Each utterance she attempted to push out was lost with another attack on her mouth.

"What are you trying to say, Princess?"

"I don't know," she breathed.

"No? No, what?"

Her arms fell limp and she slumped against the mirror when he jerked her forward and knelt, pushing her knees wide apart. One glide of his tongue over her clit and her body fully deceived her, chasing away her objections on moans and gasps.

He returned to his feet, his beard dripping with her juices and leaving her pussy aching for more. He collapsed over her, slamming a palm onto the mirror and releasing his throbbing cock with the other. Her brain barely registered the movements since her body had transformed into a rag doll, limp and willing with no mind of its own. A fact she was unable to disguise as she clung to him. His hand fell from between them and slapped the marble slab next to her when he thrust inside her. His mouth crashed onto hers, devouring her, his beard grazing her chin and spreading her sweet stickiness where it touched. His muscles flexed inside his shirt, under her palms, and his ass rocked between her legs, building a tidal wave of nerves throughout her.

On a moan, Ellis abandoned her mouth and raised above her, where she became lost in his eyes. His neck stiffened and his body shivered as if at war with itself, thrusting hard, fucking her with an intensity she had never experienced. She squeezed her eyes as wave after wave of pleasure rippled through her. Ellis stiffened under her touch and drove into her once more, emptying himself and warming her from the inside.

Her eyes fluttered open toward his face above hers, twisted in ecstasy. She raised a shaky hand to his neck, the heat scorching her palm.

His fingers dug into her flesh, jerking her body upright with his, his fingers pressing deep into her back where he held her until her breathing returned normal.

His finger glided under her chin and lifted her eyes toward his. "That pretty little tongue of yours will be our undoing." He traced her lower lip. "Take my scent to bed with you. Feel the slickness between your thighs and know you're mine."

In an instant, she was on her feet and being guided through the door, begging her legs to stay strong until she reached the bed. She twisted back in time to witness him adjust himself back into his pants and turn away.

Kiss of Power

Jewelz Baxter

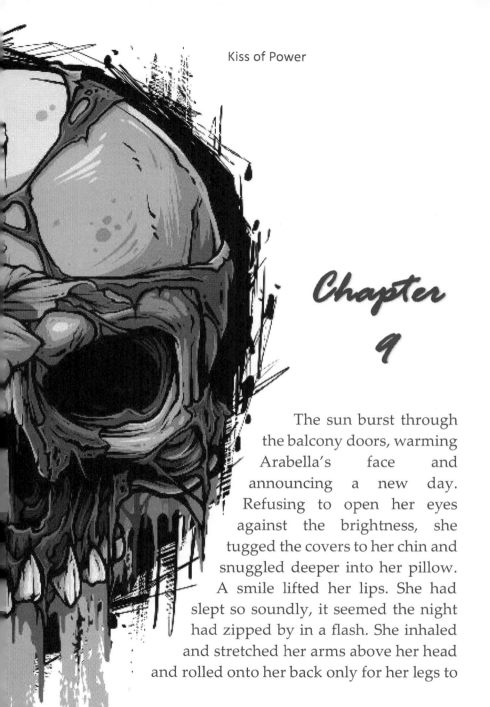

Chapter 9

The sun burst through the balcony doors, warming Arabella's face and announcing a new day. Refusing to open her eyes against the brightness, she tugged the covers to her chin and snuggled deeper into her pillow. A smile lifted her lips. She had slept so soundly, it seemed the night had zipped by in a flash. She inhaled and stretched her arms above her head and rolled onto her back only for her legs to become twisted in the robe she still wore. Suddenly, her eyes popped open. She'd fallen asleep in her robe. She threw back the covers and padded into the bathroom.

Staring into the mirror, the night before came crashing down. She tilted her head, zoning in on a single smudge on the mirror, but that was no ordinary smudge. Slowly, she lifted her hand and placed her palm in the center of his handprint. "Not a dream," she breathed.

Arabella jerked from her daze and ran to twist the lock of both doors. Her robe fell to the floor, and she stepped into the shower. Tilting back her head, she welcomed the warm water that flowed over her face and down her body, washing his scent down the drain. She closed her eyes. Damn him for kissing her, for touching her. She grabbed her shower gel, snatched the loofa from its place, and began lathering herself. How dare he think he owns her and is privileged to take advantage? He knew she was in here when he walked in.

She paused, his words echoing in her mind. All unlocked doors are fair game. Her shoulders fell and she threw back her head. She had not engaged the lock, lesson learned, but he should have walked out. Instead, he invaded her space and set her body on edge. Just staring into his eyes made her mouth go dry.

Her tongue. He'd told her to keep it inside. It had taken on a mind its own when her lips had gone dry. She squeezed her eyes. She didn't listen. She'd learned he never issued a threat that he wasn't prepared to follow through with. And she'd noticed the intensity of his eyes. And she froze.

Arabella stopped the water and fell against the smooth tile. She was doomed. As much as she hated to admit it, she was powerless to resist his advances. Well, she would dress and tell him a thing or two about their situation.

She jerked a towel from the stack near the shower and, in record time, found herself dressed and storming from her room. She darted toward the open office door and pounded her fist on the thick frame.

"Yes 'um?" His voice acknowledged her presence at the door although he never looked up from his desk.

Arabella stiffened, throwing her arms around her waist. "I hate you."

"Good to know."

"Did you hear me?" Her voice rose a bit higher.

"Clearly."

"You're a monster."

"Yes."

She popped her hands onto her hips. "Augh! Look at me."

He raised his head, dropping the papers he held flat to his desk.

"Are you sorry?" She wanted to know, or maybe she didn't, but the words flew from her without thought, filled with anger mixed with curiosity.

"For what? Falling into temptation? Giving you what you craved? Sending you to sleep alone?" He cocked his head. "No." His voice remained smooth as if this was just another casual conversation.

Anger rippled through her body. "I'm going to pack my things."

Ellis leaned back in his chair and steepled his fingers underneath his chin. "Repercussions, Princess."

"I don't care anymore. I refuse to stay here and be your sex toy."

"You're much more than that," he assured her.

Anger took over and she whirled from the door.

"Arabella?"

She paused, then snapped, "What?"

"I'll concede and offer you a deal."

She twisted only her head until he was in sight, her glare pinned on him. "Go on."

"You confess your disgust for last evening and make it to the farm, into your house, and I'll have your things packed and returned to you before nightfall."

"Be sure to launder my robe before returning it." She turned and took slow steps, listening for any objections. No sounds came from his office. Of course, he was bullying her. One more glance toward his open office door and she ran down the stairs and fled from the house.

***

The farm wasn't that far away. Plus, once she reached the farmland, it was a sure shot to the house. Then she would be rid of Ellis for good. He most likely would expect her to take the straight path behind the house and through the thicket, so she ran down the drive and turned away from the main road. She'd be home in no time.

The first thing she would do is begin her job search. She had no idea what the agreement between her father and Ellis could be. But what she did know, was she was furious with them both and planned to leave town. She had no qualms about sending money to her father for upkeep of his home, but she no longer would live there if he was agreeable to anything Ellis had propositioned.

She ran and ran, dodging limbs and obstacles, until she stood at the fence line of the back field. Movement caught her attention and she stepped onto the bottom rungs, a foot on either side of the fencepost, balancing. Her fingers still touching the top of the wooden post, she stretched to get a better view. Two men she'd never seen before worked alongside her father, preparing the ground for planting. They appeared to be working efficiently and smoothly. Her shoulders slumped and she hopped to the ground.

She'd been gone for weeks, and he appeared to be carrying on just fine. She worked from daylight till dusk, but she couldn't do the work of two men. Had Ellis hired these men? Would he fire them if she returned home? She turned and tucked her arms around her waist. All of a sudden, exhaustion set in, and her head was spinning.

Her steps were slow and mindless as she wandered the estate. She had lost track of time when she happened upon a beautifully designed garden tucked away amidst a small grove of trees. She eased into the sunlight beaming down on the hidden haven. Large blooms provided a colorful backdrop for a six-foot-tall and wide arch raining water into a bed of smooth river rock. A raised wooden bed surrounded the focal point of the space. Three tall copper feathered structures were stationed near one end of the rain wall. She moved toward the tall, slender wooden art piece with blue and green glass orbs held strategically in the center of a long slit carved into a beautiful piece of driftwood. The glass was bright and warm under her touch from the rays of the sun.

She stepped back and settled onto the long metal bench. Studying the space, she wondered who could have designed such a calming, beautiful oasis to stumble upon. Somehow, Ellis didn't come across as someone to sit in a garden to contemplate life. Or to relax. He never appeared to relax. He was all business and matter of fact, allowing very little, if any, emotions to slip out. Although, the time she has spent here had surprised her and at times confused her even more. He was a complete enigma.

Her thoughts drifted to the night before. Had she wanted him to kiss her? No. Had she wanted him to take her? No. Did she really hate him?

Okay, so maybe hate was a bit extreme. He did know how to push her buttons, and it was apparent he enjoyed that. She stared at the streams of water across the way. Could she truly place all the blame on him when she kissed him back? She shivered and leaned back, lifting one leg across the other. She refused to examine that point right now, or the fact that he was sexy as hell and sent her stomach into knots with those piercing blue eyes. No, she was not going there.

Arabella twisted and crossed her arms over the back of the seat and dropped her head onto them. The calming patter of water drops splashing over the rocks lulled her into a trance, chasing away her concerns and all tension from her body until the word faded.

A shift of the bench startled her. Sounds of the garden met her ears again, although her eyes remained closed. She waited and listened. Nothing moved or sounded odd. Must have been her imagination.

"Enjoying the garden?"

She blinked, trying to determine how long she'd sat here. Slowly, she straightened and avoided looking in Ellis's direction.

"You should experience it at night," he told her. "The accent lighting is remarkable."

She forced a glance his way to discover him concentrating on the rain wall.

"Why didn't you go to your father's? You've had plenty of time to make it."

"Did I crush your expectations of dragging me back here and locking me up?"

Ellis sighed. "I gave you specific instructions to free yourself of the agreement. You chose not to accept them."

"I accepted the challenge and ran."

"But you didn't cross the fence."

"No," she whispered, staring across the garden.

"Not to mention that you failed to tell me you were disgusted by my touch."

Arabella jerked her head, shooting him a glare, then returned her focus to the waterfall.

"What's the real reason you remain here?"

"I gave him my word that I'd stay here without question while he handled whatever it was he hesitated to enlighten me on."

"Noble of you."

"Disappointed?"

"Not in the least. Nor am I surprised. I've always suspected you were virtuous and determined. A true lady."

"And I always suspected that you were a pompous, egotistical ass."

He raised a brow. "You feel the need to use both descriptions?"

She narrowed her eyes at him. "Because you're twice as irritating."

He nodded and returned his gaze to the fountain. "So, you like my ass. Good to know."

She jumped to her feet. "You are impossible to talk to." She stormed past him and made her way back to the house.

***

Ellis remained statuesque, ankle across a knee and both arms hooked over the back of the bench lost in the rain wall as she disappeared. When the sound of her steps faded to silence, he retrieved his phone from his pocket. In seconds, it was ringing against his ear.

"Hey, boss," the voice answered.

"We need to meet," Ellis ordered.

"Where?"

"Where are you? I'll come to you."

"We're both in the south field."

"On my way." Ellis ended the call and slipped the phone back into his coat pocket. With a deep cleansing breath, he pushed to his feet and set out walking toward the south field. Visions of Arabella filled his mind, the way her body responded to him the night before, and the anger she blasted at him this morning. But she remained under his roof without a fight. A corner of his lips lifted into a lopsided grin wondering who she was really angry with—herself or him.

The fence line came into sight, along with Dawson and Tucker. Slowing to a stop next to the fence post where they waited, he nudged open his jacket and slid his hands into his pockets. "How's it going here?"

Tucker hung his head with a shake. "Boss, when you said don't be surprised at any requested task," he looked up, "I never imagined this would be on the list of responsibilities."

"I must agree," Dawson chimed in, "this is different."

"You'll get a reprieve day after tomorrow. Only for one night though."

Tucker straightened from where his arms rested on the post. "What do we need to do?"

"I'm having a small gathering that evening. I need the two of you and Gus to cover the back of the house. My guests will have their men covering the front. Usual routine. Stay out of sight and alert. The red light above the veranda will signal your dismissal."

Each man nodded and, almost in unison, told him, "Got it."

Ellis gave a curt nod in return and turned back toward the house for his next order of business — sooth Arabella's anger with something pretty. Maybe jewelry. No, she would prefer something simple and elegant with a purpose, such as his last gifts. That's it. Flowers.

He picked up his pace. By noon, she would have enough blooms to fill the window boxes on the cottage. And by the end of the day, she would be talking to him once again.

***

By that evening, just as Ellis suspected, Arabella had filled the window boxes with marigolds, and they'd enjoyed a pleasant meal. As he escorted her to her room, he stopped in the hallway. "I was considering a little dinner party. Something intimate with a few friends."

She laughed lightly, imagining him attempting to entertain anyone she knew. "You have friends?"

"Family and associates may be a more precise term."

She paused at the entrance of her bedroom and whirled on him, throwing her hands to her hips. "So you can show me off? Gloat after shoving your tongue down my throat?"

His eyes heated, burning straight into her core. She dropped her gaze away. How could the one man she despised melt away her resolve so quickly? Resolve? Her brain scoffed at her. Surely, she meant clothes. An intensely seductive aura radiated from him each time he came near, dissipating her very will . . . and her clothes.

His breath was warm and hearty, and his voice grew low, almost like a growl next to her ear. "I did, as you say, shove my tongue down your throat. Or I would have if yours hadn't been dancing the same passion. But that was only the appetizer, as I recall, because my tongue had a feast that night. Teasing right here." The tip of his tongue outlined her earlobe, forcing her eyelids to drift close. Her hands slid up his coat jacket, twisting in the lapels.

"Then here."

Shivers rippled down her body as it seemed to take control and her head eased to the side, giving access for his mouth as it travelled her neck down to her shoulder. A fingertip trailed down her chest until his touch slowed between her breasts. Her chest heaved as his words brushed her ear again. "And here."

The heat of his hand through her dress burned to the core. "But when I reached here, I shoved my tongue deep into those sweet folds and caught every single drop as I teased and suckled a certain little nub until streams of cum shot past my tongue and warmed my throat."

His teeth shot sparks through her earlobe. "But I wasn't done. I shared that sweetness with you, and you sucked every bit of it from my mouth just as that pussy of yours then sucked every drop of goodness from my dick." He lifted his head only to drop his forehead against hers.

"You recall those spasms clenching and milking my cock as you coated it over and over again?"

She forced down a swallow but found it impossible to push out a sound.

"So, yes, I shoved my tongue down your throat, but I don't gloat. I don't humiliate." He leaned more until their lips were only a breath's width apart. "I reserve the efforts of my mouth for more pleasurable things."

He straightened and dropped his arms. "Sleep well, Miss Bartel." He stepped back and spun away.

Arabella was rooted to the spot, unable to so much as look away.

"Fair warning," he began, and her head jerked toward where Ellis stood at his bedroom door, his hand resting on the doorknob. "I will kiss you again." He raised a smug brow and disappeared into his room.

Kiss of Power

Jewelz Baxter

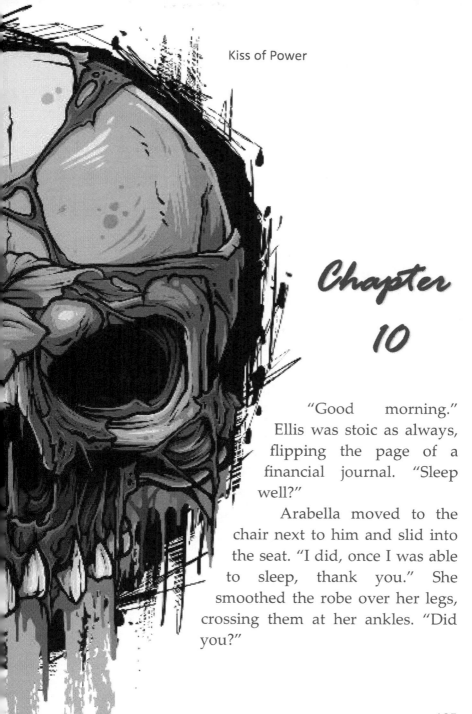

Chapter 10

"Good morning." Ellis was stoic as always, flipping the page of a financial journal. "Sleep well?"

Arabella moved to the chair next to him and slid into the seat. "I did, once I was able to sleep, thank you." She smoothed the robe over her legs, crossing them at her ankles. "Did you?"

He scanned the page that he'd not looked up from since she walked in. "Indeed, I did. With visions of soft and sweet rewards. Might I inquire what kept that lovely mind and body of yours from drifting into a sweet slumber?"

Arabella felt the heat threatening to creep in. How did he manage to twist everything into an erotically suggestive thought? "Now, that's just uncalled for." She fell against the tall, upholstered chair's back and folded her arms.

"Good morning, Miss Bartel." Mrs. Moretti walked in with a plate in each hand.

"Good morning, Mrs. Moretti. Thank you for breakfast."

"It was no trouble at all. Mr. Darby filled me in on your schedule today, and a nice meal seemed appropriate to get you started."

Her head popped toward Ellis. "Schedule?"

Ellis finally set the journal aside and looked up. "The dinner party we discussed last night."

"We didn't discuss anything last night."

He placed an arm on the table, leaning closer toward her. "Should I recount the conversation?"

Her cheeks felt as if they would burst into flames at any moment. She forced down a swallow and hoped Mrs. Moretti hadn't noticed the implications of the the exchange.

"Our flight leaves in exactly two hours. Eat and dress, then we'll leave. We're going shopping."

"Afraid to be seen in town with me here since you've kept me hostage?"

"What we're purchasing can't be found nearby. I have a consultant ready to meet with us in Dallas to assist you."

"So, now, I'm not capable of shopping for myself?" Slowly, she raised her gaze from her lap, where she smoothed out a cloth napkin to see Ellis. "Or you can't handle it yourself?"

"I am quite capable of obtaining anything I need or desire. I inform someone of what I want, and they bring it to me. Shopping is a waste of time." Another sip of coffee and he settled the mug next to his plate. "As I said, she is to assist you. If I had been positive of your evening gown preference, I would've just had it delivered."

Arabella had recently learned he didn't like to shop. The day of shopping he had previously promised, had been a day of scrolling through online shops and placing orders. But an evening gown? He had not mentioned that fact when he told her of the dinner party. Questions bounced around her mind like dice tumbling to see which would win the chance to be asked first.

"I realize your free spirit prefers the informal lifestyle over restricted and ritual situations."

Arabella's eyes darted toward Ellis as she slid another bite from her fork. All the dice in her head just landed the same number, battling to spill from her. Instead, she remained silent.

"I'm not inferring that you're not capable of such events but that you don't prefer them."

He was right. She acknowledged this with a slight nod and took another bite.

"We grow by experiencing new things. I dare say this will be a growing experience for us both."

***

Arabella stood in front of the mirrored wall, smoothing her hands down her dress. She felt like the princess that Ellis called her. From the elegant comb holding her twisted hair in place, down to her toes that matched her perfectly manicured nails.

She had attended dinners before and socialized at her job before deciding to move back and run the farm with her father. But nothing she'd experienced would compare to the coming event she imagined.

One last check of her hair and she turned toward the door when Ellis stepped into the room. "Breathtaking."

"Thank you."

"Ready to greet our guests?"

She slipped her hand into the crook of his elbow, and they headed down the stairs together.

"You two look lovely," Mrs. Moretti boasted.

"Thank you," Arabella replied, descending the last of the stairs. She glanced toward the table Mrs. Moretti had elegantly set before disappearing into the kitchen. She turned toward Ellis. "Ready to gloat?"

"Ready to behave?"

"I guess we'll see."

Ellis grinned. "So we shall."

The entrance door swung open, bringing Conner and Alex into sight as they walked in. "You two do know my home is equipped with a doorbell," Ellis chastised.

Alex closed the door with a click and grinned. "Yeah. And it's a lovely melody of chimes. And loud."

Conner stepped forward. "Arabella, you look lovely this evening."

"Thank you, Conner."

"Ah." Alex cocked his head, closing the gap between him and where the others stood, obviously studying Ellis and Arabella standing next to each other. "I see it now."

Arabella snapped her head toward Ellis.

"What?" Ellis blurted.

Alex slowly nodded, taking his time to answer his brother. "I now see why you stay here, Arabella. To make him look good." The back of his hand thudded against Ellis's chest as he stepped past them and toward the great room. "Out of your entire entourage, I'd say she's your best decision. How much do you pay her to improve your image?"

A quick laugh tumbled from Arabella, and her grip on Ellis's arm tightened when his chest rumbled next to her with a low growl.

Conner turned toward Alex at the wet bar. "A shot to begin the evening? I'm in." He joined him and took the filled shot glass from Alex and waited for him to fill another. "Ellis?"

"There's still time for you to leave before our guests arrive," Ellis replied and squeezed her hand before stepping away. "I can do this without the two of you."

"Now, you know we're not going to let you have all the fun." Alex met Ellis midway through the room with a shot for Ellis and himself. Ellis accepted, and Conner joined them.

"To the team together again," Conner toasted.

Arabella remained by the large arched opening, watching the three men. Well, mainly Ellis. His presence demanded her attention, strong and commanding, something she couldn't deny very much appealed to her. Then there was Conner, the quiet one. He appeared to be solemn and always in deep thought. Somewhat like Ellis but on a smaller scale. Her focus moved to Alex, the complete opposite of the other two, always seeking the humor in things. A smile lifted her lips, and she studied Ellis again. If she didn't know better, she would have sworn the rumble she'd heard from Ellis had a hint of jealousy in it.

Their voices faded away, leaving her watching as they silently returned the empty glasses to the bar just as musical chimes filled the home. Arabella sucked in a breath and her thoughts returned to the night's event. It was apparent this was an important dinner for Ellis, and she wondered how long this soiree had actually been planned. Plus, she had been given no hints as to the guest list.

Ellis greeted each guest as they arrived one by one and introduced her. Antonio Luis Polito and his wife, Francesca. Then, Jackson Salvador and his date, Whiskey Rivers. She had not been in a room with this many tuxes since her senior prom many years ago. The spectacular evening gowns of their guests also reinforced her appreciation for the trip to Dallas.

They advanced into the great room, filling the space with lighthearted conversation. Arabella had always managed social functions with strangers, but somehow this felt different. Maybe the rigid atmosphere. Maybe the fact that Ellis's presence seemed more assertive than normal. Or it could have been that his eyes were constantly on her. She wasn't sure what, but she was positive this dinner was more than Ellis had led her to believe. She focused on the conversation, and just as the tension began to fade, dinner was announced and they were escorted to the small dining room. Caught off guard, Ellis pulled back her chair, seating her at the opposite end of the table, facing him.

Dinner was phenomenal, each course a special treat as she grew to know more and more about their guests. No, not their guests. His guests. Realization of where she had heard each of their names crashed in about time dessert was served. She felt her mind exploding as she forced her features to remain pleasant and hid that fact away before surprisingly enjoying the rest of the evening.

***

Ellis bid their guests goodbye with Arabella by his side. Two vehicles faded into the dark along the driveway as he stepped back and closed the door. "You handled that beautifully and won them over." Her skin was soft as he glided a finger underneath her chin. "Just as I knew you would."

Her smile appeared genuine, and he found himself aching to have her cast a smile like that meant for him. Just as she had the day she'd called him perfect. Even if it was only for the moment before he shattered that opinion, he held that memory locked away. "Go get comfortable." He dropped his hand away and watched her spin and lift the hem of her gown.

He tugged on his bow tie, admiring the subtle sway of Arabella's hips as she disappeared up the staircase. His tie dangled over his shoulders as he released the topmost button of his dress shirt and turned toward the great room.

"I love watching you work a room." Alex spun and handed him a drink.

"So, D'Angelo has been run out of territories to fall into ours," Conner noted.

Ellis dropped into a seat and crossed an ankle over his knee. He threw an arm across the back of the sofa and gave a nod.

"What do you propose?" Conner asked.

"He's on full radar now in two states, but his luck has run out with us," Ellis announced.

"Explains now why he had eyes on Bartel's land. Take the girl, force him to sell, build his empire next to you, and take you out." Conner guessed.

"We have our presence well known at the farm now. Let him know the girl's protected by you and he may slink away." Alex grinned. "Or I'll just take him out now."

After a moment of silence, Conner cocked his head. "He turned up at an opportune time for you."

"Most opportune. A well-played surprise," Ellis admitted.

Alex threw glances between Ellis and Conner. "What are you saying?"

Conner leaned in, dropping both elbows on his knees, cradling his tumbler. "How long have you planned this?"

"A month after moving back," Ellis confessed.

Conner dropped his head with a shake and a chuckle. "Why?"

"I need an heir." The words rolled out matter-of-factly, but his heart laughed.

"You could've had a wife at any point who was willing to do anything for you. You're the boss. You snap your fingers and they run," Alex said.

"I don't want a wife."

Conner narrowed his eyes on his brother. "So, you orchestrated the opportunity to hold this girl for collateral and have your kid for over a year?"

"She's loyal, intelligent, dependable, and discreet."

"It would've been easier to seduce her a year ago," Conner suggested.

"She despises me."

"That very well may be." Conner leaned to the side, stretching to peer past the staircase. "She just bolted through the back door."

"I'll catch her at the fence. She'll stand there for some time, deciding how to pass through the barbed wire without damaging her dress." Ellis's demeanor remained calm as he took his time emptying his tumbler. He placed his glass on the end table and stood with a sigh.

Alex jumped to his feet and moved face to face with Ellis, his palm pressing the center of his chest. "Just as I suspected. Our father failed to take your heart completely. I believe there's a faint beat inside you."

"He failed at many things." Ellis's eyes narrowed. "I won't." Ellis stepped around him. "As enlightening as this evening has been, it has come to an end."

"Go, get your girl," Conner called out. "We'll see ourselves out."

Ellis gave a nod and strolled out into the night air.

Jewelz Baxter

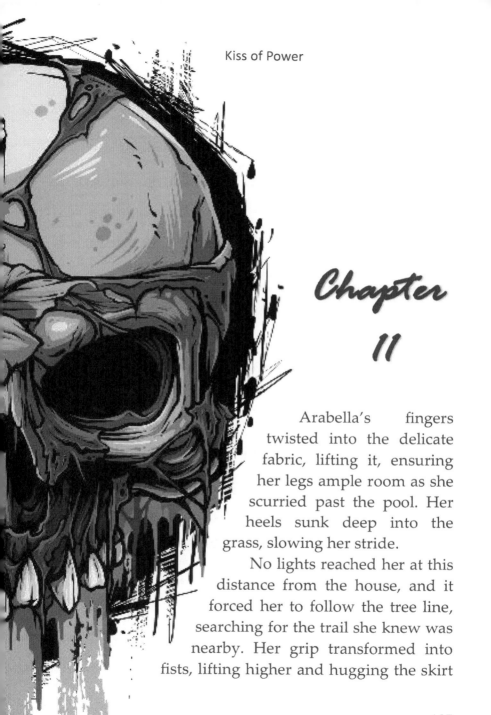

Chapter 11

Arabella's fingers twisted into the delicate fabric, lifting it, ensuring her legs ample room as she scurried past the pool. Her heels sunk deep into the grass, slowing her stride.

No lights reached her at this distance from the house, and it forced her to follow the tree line, searching for the trail she knew was nearby. Her grip transformed into fists, lifting higher and hugging the skirt to her body. The scant moonlight disappeared, bringing an eerie chill to swirl about her and quicken her pace.

The breath she'd been holding escaped, carrying tension from her shoulders as she pulled to a stop and released the grip on her dinner gown. The cool metal was a comfort beneath her fingers. Keeping her focus on the building in the far distance, she instinctively curled her hands around the wire strands without touching a barb.

"Going somewhere?"

Arabella jolted and whirled toward Ellis. The darkness gave no indication of his features or mood, and as always, his posture was rigid. His arms folded over his chest, his silence demanded a response.

"Home."

He stepped forward and reached for her hand.

She pulled her arms close to her body, tucking them over her waist. "Do you know who those people were?"

"They were my guests." He paused for only an instant then corrected. "*Our* guests."

"No, no, no. Not mine. I've heard of them. I heard you address Antonio Luis Polito as Lupo." Her eyes rounded. "He's a mafia boss from down south, and Jackson Salvador is a Texas mafia boss. Both are well known. Are you one of them? Are the stories I've heard true? Is that what you are?"

"This is the role I've been trained for my entire life. I can't change that. This is who I am."

"I believed my father when he told me you weren't like your father. Are you telling me he lied to me all these years?"

"I'm not my father. Stories are just that, stories. You must live your own life and make your own conclusions."

"What does that mean?"

"Judge me for my own actions, not my station."

"Well, I don't enjoy that sort of company."

"Were they rude to you?"

"No."

"Were the ladies unbecoming to you?"

"No."

"Did someone make you feel uncomfortable?"

"Yes."

"I'll handle them, and there will be no need to see them again."

"Good. It was you. I'm going home now." She turned back toward the fence.

"Home is this way, Princess. I know you're cold, so let's get you inside and warmed up."

"You're still not touching me." She jerked from his reach and could have sworn a silent chuckle rumbled through his chest. She cut a look toward him, but the darkness still protected him. She accepted his jacket and tugged it close as he turned her and guided her back through the dark, leafy tunnel.

***

Arabella threw her bedroom door closed and stretched to reach the zipper of her dress. Maybe if she just put this night behind her, she could reflect on the implications more clearly tomorrow. She shimmied out of her dress, letting it slide to the floor, and stepped out. The door clicked loudly behind her, and she whirled toward it. As quick as she could move, she bent and snatched the clothing from the floor, clutching it to her bare breasts.

Ellis stood just inside her room. "Come here."

"No." Her chest heaved as he approached, his steps slow and determined. Inches apart, her fist collided against the solid wall of his chest. In one swift motion, and before she could react, her gown crumpled to the floor and her wrists were bound tightly in his grip.

"Stop treating me like a child!"

"Stop acting like one."

"I know what I know. Those are the same sort my father fought to keep his land from when the rest of the town was being run out of business."

He jerked her to his chest. "If the world was truly as simple and transparent as you perceive it to be, it would be a much better place. But the world is evil, a place where we do what we must to survive."

Her breath grew so deep that her breasts grazed the smoothness of his shirt, tightening and setting her nipples on edge.

Cursing herself for not removing her shoes first, she stumbled when he twisted them. But then again, maybe she could stab it into his foot. He deserved that, didn't he? One second, she was calculating retribution, and the next, she was being slung over his knee as his shoe pressed into the mattress.

She jerked, unable to loosen his tight grip on her wrists that hung in front of him. Her belly caved to the pressure against his thigh with every kick of her feet. He slapped her ass, and she froze, the sting radiating throughout her bottom.

"Stop fighting me." His hand landed on her ass again.

Her squeal was involuntary, and she regretted it the instant it spilled out. She squeezed her eyes and clenched her jaw. She would submit, then maybe he would stop. Or at least that's what she told herself, although deep down, she knew better.

The warmth of his palm circling her round bottom began to seep in, leading her body to relax. And without warning, he smacked her again.

She could feel her face twisting. Don't fight. Don't fight. The warning echoed through her mind.

He warmed her cheek again and smacked it a bit harder this time.

"Are you going to run again?"

Her mind screamed no, but the protest was captured in her head. Another smack on her ass and she squirmed against him more.

"Are you going to lie to me?"

Again, her words bounced around her head, refusing to leave.

"Think I treat you like a child?"

The words remained stuck in her throat. She jerked her head side to side, but still no words tumbled out.

"If I treated you like a child, I wouldn't do this."

Her breath caught at the touch of his finger slipping underneath the thin silky material she was sure had become buried deep between her ass cheeks from her struggling.

He nudged her leg. "Open up." His fingers slid forward and across her folds to circle her clit. "Oh, somebody's turned on."

"You're twisted."

"And you're wet." He slowly retraced his path, sliding his fingertips inside her, then pulling his hand from her thong. He tugged her arms, bringing her to her feet and face to face with him.

Her eyes darted to his to witness his finger sliding across his tongue. "Still sweet." His eyes grew dark, burning away her resistance.

"Open up."

She shook her head.

"Ah ah ah. Open up."

Her body deceived her as if she were hypnotized by his voice, controlled by his eyes. Her lips parted slightly but enough for his finger to slide between them and across her tongue. "Like that? That's how you taste. Like perfection. But you know that, don't you?"

He moved so fast, she barely registered his finger leaving her lips and twisting in her hair before his mouth crashed onto hers, forceful and domineering. And just as quick, her lips were abandoned.

Her body lurched forward, begging his mouth back onto hers.

His eyes narrowed. "But you don't want me touching you."

The room felt as if it were spinning, but it was her instead. Her back crashed against his chest, the small buttons of his shirt pressing into her spine. Bristles of roughness teased her neck as the voice lulled her ear.

"But you like my kisses. You quite enjoy my lips on your lips and your body."

She swallowed, knowing she'd lost the battle. Her skin tingled under his touch, gathering at her core.

"Tell me, Princess, what happens when I kiss you? Do you go to sleep with my name on your lips? Do you have a dirty little secret tucked away that you pull out and dance with?" His hand slipped around hers, guiding it down her chest and slowly over her stomach. "Or do you just take care of business yourself?" Her hand was now pressed between the soaked material and his palm that manipulated hers.

If not for his arm around her waist, she surely would have crumpled to the floor. Her eyelids drifted closed, and her head dropped back against his shoulder.

Their hands slid back to her belly. "Or do you prefer skin to skin?" His whisper reverberated throughout her body that no longer belonged to her.

Her palm was warm where it slid along her skin and dipped below the material. Her hand and fingers moved like a marionette being orchestrated for her pleasure, and her moan sounded foreign as if it did not slip from her own lips.

"Ah. That's what you prefer. Now if I were to touch you, I would spread a little of that goodness."

Arabella was lost. A fog had claimed her brain and ripples of pleasure began rolling through her body, threatening to build with intensity. The wetness from her finger circled her pebbled bud, tightening it like a rosy diamond.

"But that's just what I'd do." His beard teased her back from one side to the other. "But you prefer I not touch you."

She stumbled again at the loss of his hands as the heat of his body faded.

"Good night." His voice sounded like a faint echo from across the room.

The room was scorching. Or was that her? Her skin burned and her core ached. She wanted to hate him. But he was right, his voice wooed her and his touch set her on fire. His eyes melted her, and his dominance erased her will.

As much as she hated that, she couldn't control it. She stood at the foot of her bed, silently cursing him for teasing her. She begged her heart to slow, but it was a lost cause. Each thought of him burned deeper, setting her heart to beat faster and heavier.

She crawled onto the bed and twisted, falling backward onto her pillow. Her eyes fell shut and her fingertips retraced his manipulations as his voice replayed in her head.

The heel of her shoe dug into the mattress, making way to her playground. She reached to her nipple begging attention while her opposite fingers crept into the thong, dancing to the rhythm he had stroked her pussy.

Waves rolled, sending hot sparks to every nerve in her body, building and spreading until her desire became a single sensation waiting to explode. Ellis filled her mind and her hand flattened to squeeze herself as he had. She hung on the edge, teetering between torment and ecstasy. Her eyes popped open, staring straight at him standing in the doorway, his shoulder supporting him against the wall. She couldn't look away. Her hands couldn't stop, just as she couldn't stop his name from rolling from her tongue.

He jerked the end of his tie and slung it across the room. His shirt drifted open as he stalked closer.

Abandoning her breast, she reached for him, yearning to run her fingers through the curls on his chest. She ached to feel them brushing against her skin. They locked eyes, and his bright blue had faded to a steel gray, barely visible from the darkness that filled them.

"Show me. Let me watch." His words were electric shooting through her, surging out of control. "That's it." His praise stoked the fire. The sound of his zipper was music ripping through the air. His eyes never strayed from hers as he jerked open his pants, freeing his cock that bulged from the top of his waistband. He wrapped his hand around himself.

Arabella took it all in. Every detail. Every movement. Every stroke that he made, she felt it and fell into rhythm with him. Her fingers plunged in and curled into that sweet spot, igniting an explosion so raw and intense, her body arched from the bed with his name again on her lips.

The instant her back returned to the mattress, he was above her. His jaw ticked and the veins of his neck appeared as if they would burst at any moment. She was transfixed, but she wouldn't have moved even if she could.

Hot, thick cum shot onto her and oozed between her breasts and down her belly, burning her skin more than the heat of her own desire had. He lurched forward, pressing his palms into the pillow framing her head. His eyes bore into hers, dark and mesmerizing, a look like none she'd seen before.

One hand left the bed and brushed her cheek a moment before the second hand pushed from the pillow, returning him to his full height. Then, without a word, he turned and disappeared from the room.

Jewelz Baxter

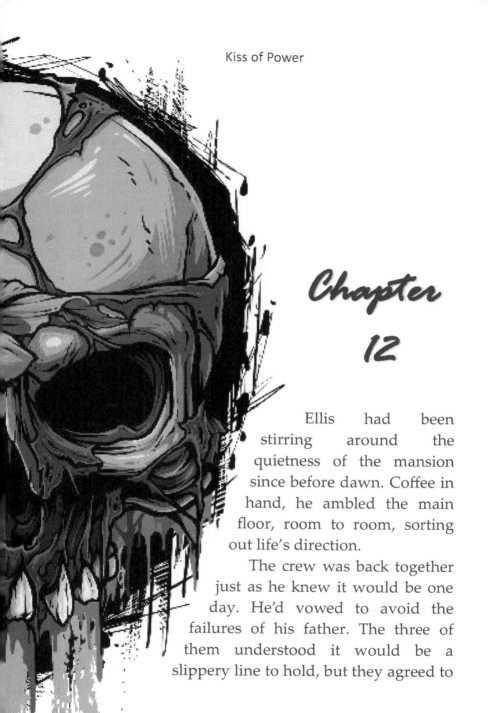

Chapter 12

Ellis had been stirring around the quietness of the mansion since before dawn. Coffee in hand, he ambled the main floor, room to room, sorting out life's direction.

The crew was back together just as he knew it would be one day. He'd vowed to avoid the failures of his father. The three of them understood it would be a slippery line to hold, but they agreed to the challenge. He was confident in the growing success, although he reigned in any visible excitement for the task.

His mind flew back to Arabella. She'd enchanted their guests, staking her place as mistress of the manor. He succumbed to the lopsided lift of his lips as he stared toward the first streaks of orange announcing the day. She was more of a delight than he had expected. Her spirit was refreshing. And the way she melted to his will . . . he huffed a laugh and downed the final bit of his coffee. Priceless, he decided. She was priceless.

He returned to the kitchen and placed his mug next to the coffee pot. He would need more, but for now, he had something more pressing.

Ellis fumbled around the kitchen. He had watched Mrs. Moretti enough times, this should be no problem. A skillet, eggs, butter, seasoning, juice, bagels. He scanned over the items collected on the countertop. No problem. He twisted the knob, sending the heat to the skillet, and began with the eggs. Twenty minutes later, with three attempts landing in the trash, he scooped perfect and fluffy scrambled eggs onto a plate. He grabbed the bagel, searching the countertop for the toaster he knew he owned. Nowhere in sight. Cabinet doors flew open and slammed closed as he searched each one. Finally, he discovered its spot, pulled it to the island, and plugged it in, dropping the open bagel inside.

With the eggs and a glass of juice on a tray, he added the toasted bagel to the plate. Leaving the mess behind, he headed up the stairs.

He bumped open her door and walked straight to her bed. "Good morning." Ellis placed the breakfast tray next to Arabella as she stretched awake. A step backward and he dropped into the chair facing her.

She scooted to sit against the headboard, pulling the sheet over her chest. "What's this?"

"I thought you might enjoy a little pampering today."

She shot him a quick look of irritation but moved the tray onto her lap.

"I appreciate the level of sophistication you displayed at the dinner party. That could have gone one-eighty if you had so chosen. I thank you."

"Throw the good girl a bone and she'll behave. Is that it?"

His lip twitched but never lifted into a smile.

"Whatever conflict we have is private," she assured him. "They know you, they must know what an evil person you are, but they came to enjoy the evening." She grinned. "Just knowing you were sweating every moment, waiting for my mouth to take over, was satisfying enough."

"I never doubted for a moment the graceful way you would finesse our guests. You shared an event of mine, so I, in turn, would like to treat you to a day of your choosing."

Arabella never looked up as her shoulders fell. "How long do you plan to keep me here?"

"I imagine my home has bored you with limited activities and interaction."

"Boring is a bit extreme. I'm accustomed to being active most of the day. Cleaning, working in the yard or fields. Cooking. I've enjoyed the flower garden, but I feel useless here."

"You're far from useless. If you desire, we can discuss minor changes to the responsibilities of running the household. But for today, what's your pleasure? What would a normal day look like for you away from the farm?"

"I would love to get out of the house. Maybe the library again. I've read those books and could exchange them out for new ones."

"Absolutely. Take your time getting dressed. When you come downstairs, I'll have a car ready to take us any place you like."

***

The tap of Arabella's heels on the staircase announced her arrival, bringing Ellis out from the great room. She was stunning. He took her in from her low strappy heels, up the sage green dress that hugged her like a second skin, to her averted eyes. He stepped forward, meeting her at the base of the banister. "You look lovely."

"Thank you." Her words came out weak, and she seemed to be focused on the floor before her.

He cocked his head and held out the two thrillers that she'd chosen for him. "I'll need a new one also."

"You've read them?"

"I did, and I quite enjoyed them both." He closed the space between them. "But not as much as I enjoyed your performance last evening."

Arabella pulled in a breath. It was so slight, but he noticed it as she moved to step around him. His hand shot out, catching her. If not for the books she clutched against her chest, he would have held her close. Instead, he reached out and glided his fingers across her cheek and underneath her chin. Her skin was so soft and warm. "Look at me." He lifted slowly, watching her focus remain away from him. "You have not one thing to be embarrassed about. You are a remarkable woman. Don't ever allow anything to make you question that. Stand tall and own it. Be proud that you, and you alone, have the ability to bring me to my knees."

Slowly, her eyes lifted to his.

"And that's exactly what you did last night." His lips tasted hers for a soft moment before he turned and placed her hand in the crook of his arm. "Now, let's get my brazen huzzy to the library."

Arabella's hip collided with his, igniting a grin that Ellis kept hidden.

***

Ellis leaned his back against the side of the car, mesmerized as always by the sway of Arabella's hips. She stopped and spun midway to the building, forcing him from his trance.

"Are you coming in?"

He pushed from the car and tucked his hands into his pockets as he closed the gap between them. "You need my assistance to find smutty books so you can imagine doing twisted things to me?"

"Oh please, I just figured it would be easier for you to stare at my butt from inside where I'd be than out here imagining it." She jerked to a halt as he pulled open the door to the building. "By the way, I don't imagine doing anything to you." Her brows lifted as she shot him a warning look.

He leaned near as she stepped past. "Good to know. You prefer I do those things to you. Plus, no need to imagine when you can recall on memories." He felt the chill bumps spread over her skin as he guided her through the door. The day may not be so boring after all.

Ellis took the same seat he did before as she searched the shelves for new worlds to fall into. Twenty minutes later, she stood facing him with her selections in hand. "I'm ready."

With a nod, he stood and walked with her to the front desk as she mindlessly went through the process of borrowing the small stack. "What would you like to do next?" he asked, pulling open the door.

Arabella stepped into the sunlight and smiled, titling her face toward the brightness. "How about the park?"

"The city park?"

"Yes."

"We have acres to lose yourself in and a nice portion of beautifully sculpted greenery. Does that not interest you?"

"I love seeing the people. Watching the kids run around playing and the mothers enticing the squirrels to come close enough for the little ones to get a look at."

Ellis raised his brows with a shake of his head. "To the park then."

"We need to stop at the dollar store first."

Ellis jerked to a halt, his fingers wrapped around the car door handle. "Excuse me?"

"I'll pick up a blanket to sit on. Unless you wish to return to the house and I run in and get mine."

"You'll pick up nothing." He pulled open the door and slid in after her. "Gus, to the dollar store." Ellis narrowed his eyes at the reflection in the rearview mirror, silencing the slight chuckle from his driver. He had never once set foot in this establishment. A national chain store filled with inexpensive necessities was not on his list of places to do business. Personal business or "advisement" business.

Gus drove across the road and parked next to the brightly painted building. "Sir, would you like for me take care of the purchase?"

"No, Gus. Miss Bartel would like to view their blankets. We'll return shortly."

"Yes, sir."

Ellis stepped to the ground and rolled his shoulders. This day was going downhill quickly. Without a word, he accompanied Arabella inside and waited as she made her choices. Yes, choices. He should have known she would be unable to leave this place with only one item. Holding a blanket, a sun hat, a baseball cap, two bottles of water, and a bag to carry all her purchases, he escorted her back to the SUV.

Arabella's voice was faint as he returned to his place next to her. His lips parted to ask her what she said, but then he glanced up. Gus's grin overshadowed

Arabella's request. "To the park," he commanded with an extra glare to the driver.

"To the park," Gus repeated and pulled onto the road.

During the drive to the park, Arabella removed the tags from all their purchases, discarding them into the plastic store bag, then placed the items into the cute blue and white striped bag she'd discovered in the store. The short twenty-minute drive passed in no time, and they were veering into the park and bypassing the designated parking lot. Gus drove farther in before stopping.

Arabella hopped from the SUV onto the blacktop of the drive meandering throughout the park. She draped the rope handles over her shoulder and inhaled deeply as she looked around. Spring was in full swing, amplifying the mixture of sweet scents filling the air.

She stepped away as Ellis moved to the driver's window. Their conversation was a low drum in her ear as she zeroed in on the laughter of the children across the playground as they chased one another around a jungle gym.

"Shall we?"

His touch warmed her back more than the sun when he appeared next to her. She twisted to face him and waited for the hum of the vehicle to fade away.

"Are you sure you're not secretly hating this to make me pay in some twisted way later?"

She was not amiss to the lopsided grin that passed over Ellis's lips.

"Now, there's an idea." Ellis's hand abandoned her side and caught her fingers. "But no, I speak my mind and I promised a day of your choosing."

A lightness bubbled up in Arabella's chest, erupting in a smile. "Let's walk down to the water. Sometimes the geese are about."

"Lead the way."

After a short trek on the single lane roadway, the pond became clear. Geese waddled among the trees shading the edge of the water. A rocky slope separated them from the pier stretching toward the center of the pond. She pulled to a stop. "Obviously not the best footwear for the park."

"Then we'll make another trip to see the geese better," he offered.

"When I had time, I loved coming here for a picnic and sharing my breadcrumbs with them." Arabella laughed. "Some of them are stingy and they fight over them." She jerked toward Ellis. "We could so have a picnic here one day. I can prepare sandwiches for a lunch."

Arabella caught her breath. What did she just do? Just this morning she was hoping, no, she was nearly ready to plead to go home soon. Now, she offered a plan for a future date with this man.

"We can have one today," Ellis offered.

Her lips parted and she jerked toward Ellis. "Huh? What?"

"A picnic."

Arabella felt her head bouncing in understanding, but her brain had not quite wrapped around the fact she just talked like they had a future together. "I can have something put together in no time and be back here quick."

"I draw the line at returning home to prepare a couple of sandwiches. I'll have Gus bring a spread." He pulled his phone from his pocket and rattled off an order to be delivered at a specific time as they rerouted their walk deeper into the park.

Past the largest playground area and tennis courts, Ellis chose a spot underneath a tree. Arabella glanced around them. Near enough to witness the continuous action of the parkgoers but farther past the crowd to relax. Perfect. She tugged the blanket from the bag, releasing it when Ellis reached for it.

She settled on her knees, rolled to sit on her hip, and reached for her shoes.

Ellis said nothing but dropped to his heels next to her and brushed away her hands. His large fingers worked like magic, manipulating the small buckle around her ankles. Fingers that amazed her. Took her to places she never imagined. She shook her head and straightened.

"Everything all right?"

She snapped her gaze to his. He cocked his head, his forehead wrinkled with confusion. No, she wasn't okay. What was happening to her today? First, future plans. Now, recalling images of his hands on her. She forced a smile. "Everything is perfect."

His eyes narrowed.

"Really. I'm just taken by surprise, that's all. I never imagined you a gentleman."

"Fair."

Arabella watched as he stretched out beside her and tucked his elbow underneath his side, facing her. "What did you decide to read here?"

She pulled a book from the bag and held the cover up for him to see. *Laying Brick* by Jewelz Baxter. She stretched out on her stomach, resting on her elbows with the book open in front of her.

"Advice on getting laid?" Ellis joked.

Arabella rolled her eyes. Of course, his mind would go there. She dropped the paperback to the blanket, the edge still in her fingertips. "Obviously, it has a double meaning. I've read the other two books about Brick and Nealy. They're so sweet together. Nothing raunchy or drastic."

Ellis leaned, examining the cover again. "What is that skull logo?"

Arabella twisted the cover toward her. "That's the MC logo of the motorcycle club that Brick belongs to."

Ellis cocked a brow. "A motorcycle club book with no sex? Really?"

Men. Arabella sighed. Everything had to be connected to sex. "Of course, they have sex. They're married now. But it's sweet and . . ." Her eyelids drifted closed. How could she explain this? Popping her eyes open toward Ellis, she explained, "Theirs is a love story. There's a difference. They discovered love in an unlikely place and—"

Ellis cut in. "What unlikely place? A public park filled with families?" He glanced around them. "I could get into that. I hear there are walking paths. Why don't we take a stroll?"

"No. That's not what I meant. Not like an actual place, like pinning her to the lavatory and—"

"And what? Eating that pussy like a pro? Letting her know what heaven she now lives in?"

Arabella stared. Words fled from her mind. He could be so sweet at times, then the beast of crudeness popped his head into the conversation at the most unexpected times. But really, what should she expect from the man who . . . who . . . she dropped her head. Who did exactly what he said.

"Sounds like a man after my own heart. Shall I read this book to you?"

Arabella jolted. Her head popped up with eyes growing wide and searching Ellis's. "I don't think so."

Ellis's eyes emanated mischief as he slipped the paperback from her hands. He rolled onto his back and opened his arm, summoning her to his side.

Arabella's hesitation brought a demanding glare from him. "Princess, I'm breathless to hear how this ruthless biker who has captured your heart gets his jollies."

A shiver of anticipation shot through her and she wiggled, keeping her dress around her legs as she eased onto his shoulder. His arm closed around her and he opened the book. Should we wager on the outcome of this tale?"

"No."

"I propose whatever actions take place between these pages, we experiment with tonight."

"I dare say, you can't be that sweet."

"Challenge accepted." He lifted the tome to eye level and began reading.

Arabella listened. Mesmerized by his voice and lost in the slow and constant transformation of the white whisps floating through the green canopy above, she fell into the story. The antics and sweet banter of the couple filled her with smiles. By the slight change in Ellis's voice at certain points, he found the interaction amusing also.

"*Go. Shower.*" Ellis continued reading aloud. *Brick's hand slid from her hair, between her shoulders, down to the curve of her ass lifting, urging her body to move up the steps. She looked back when his hand fell away and at his nod, she turned and continued towards the bedroom.*

"See," Arabella spoke up. "He just sent her to bed alone."

Ellis hesitated, and she heard the flip of a page. Scanning ahead, no doubt. Then a rumble shook his chest and the page flipped back. His voice seemed a bit lighter as he continued the line of events.

The page flipped again and he paused. Arabella tilted back her head to be met with a smirk. "Ready?" he asked. At her nod, he refocused on the words filling the page.

"*What are you doing?*" *Brick asked, rolling his head towards her. His eyes dark and searching hers.* "*Loving my man.*"

"*Sweet. Been through this.*"

Nealy's sweet smile faded, her eyes turning dark and determined. Straightening, she pulled his hand from her wrist and continued reaching past that patch of hair her fingers were in. He pinned her with a look she knew all too well, bringing a wicked smile to her lips. Dropping her head, she peppered kisses over his chest. Trailing down his body, her tongue played and teased until she knelt next to his legs. His hand twisted in her hair bringing up her head. Locking eyes with him, she only grinned and reached to tug the denim lower that hid her desire.

Arabella's eyes popped. Nealy hadn't been aggressive in the other two books. She squeezed her eyes. Oh, the ideas that Ellis must be collecting. No, rephrase that. He needed no prompt for ideas. But he would be expecting this later if he tried to enforce his little so-called wager. She tuned back into his voice that had now transformed into a deep and sultry tone.

His hand gripping one side and both of hers pulling the other, his jeans quickly landed next to his boots. Maneuvering herself between his knees, she glanced up once again seeking out his eyes and licked her lips as she dropped to sit on her feet curled underneath her. Beginning with his legs, she massaged every muscle of his thighs with fingertips and tongue. Moving her way up over his hips to his rock-hard stomach, she teased the sensitive skin around his manhood, never touching it. With a quick tug of the towel's edge, it slid to her waist as she rose to her knees continuing her sensual exploration of his body. Fingertips admiring muscles. Tongue tracing tattoos. Tingles filling her body when her fingers ran through the dark curls tickling her palms. He watched. Both arms now tucked behind his head. His eyes dark and narrowed, he followed her every movement. Her every expression. He couldn't tear his focus from her if he had wanted. She was so damn sexy. Leaning closer, her breasts grazed each side of his erection as she lowered herself back to rest on her feet. Glancing up, she locked eyes with him and leaned in. Slowly tracing her tongue along the veins, a moan escaped him bringing a smile to her before placing her lips on him and taking him in. The slow and steady rhythm was intoxicating, but when her tongue swirled the tip, it was his undoing.

Ellis paused. "Oh, tonight sounds promising."

"I'm not doing that," Arabella blurted.

"Let's see how he managed his luck." Ellis dove back into the story until the final page then dropped it onto his chest. "As I said, a man after my own heart."

Arabella shot up, glaring down at Ellis. "He manipulated her!"

"Yes, he did. And she ravaged him because of it. Smart man." His eyes searched out hers. "Did you not say that they were sweet and adorable?"

She glanced toward her lap. "Yes."

"And you're not one bit disgusted by how he worked the situation. You actually regarded it as sweet."

Arabella's lips parted to speak but nothing came. He was not wrong. Brick had stolen her heart, and she couldn't blame him.

"My evening has taken an unexpected, and very much anticipated, turn for the better."

She sucked in a breath to rebut him but lost her chance when his phone buzzed.

He pulled it from his pocket and glanced at the screen. "You're saved by lunch." He swiped the screen and proceeded to give Gus directions to their location. Within minutes, Ellis was retrieving a large bag from the passenger seat of the SUV and carrying it to the blanket.

In minutes, they were sitting across from each other enjoying subs, chips, and soft drinks. Although the conversation remained light and sparse, Arabella couldn't shake the erotic story and the insinuations from Ellis.

"You know," Ellis's voice derailed her train of thought, "I believe if we venture past the caboose that sits behind the tennis courts, we'll be able to reach the pond by a slighter slope and less gravel for you to traverse."

Arabella twisted, combing back the strands of hair the wind had taken command of. Across the blacktop path and past the two lively tennis courts, she examined another path leading to the faded red caboose. She'd noticed it each time she visited but had never ventured down it. Flat green terrain spread out from the retired train car in all directions. "I would like that." She twisted back.

Ellis broke a few pieces of crust from his lunch and dropped them onto the wrapper. "For your geese and ducks."

She smiled and followed suit, adding to the collection until nothing was left of the meal other than the saved bits. "That was nice. Thank you."

She leaned to her side, dropping a palm to the blanket and studying Ellis. He sat with a knee raised and his arm resting atop it. Even at a picnic, he managed to resemble a business ad for smug confidence. "You realize the sun is out."

He glanced toward the sky. "So it is."

"Aren't you uncomfortable in a full suit in this heat?"

"I've managed in more extreme temps than this."

"Do you ever dress down?"

"Never. Appearances are the first thing one notices about you. In my line, I must always appear at my best."

Arabella dropped her head to the side and twisted her lips, scouring her memory. He was right. Not once, other than the day by the pool, had he remotely attempted to relax. That was at her insistence and not in public. She rolled to her knees and closed the space between them. With a smile, she reached for his tie and worked the knot.

"What's in that head of yours?"

She wrinkled her nose. "I would like to see you a bit more comfortable."

"Why is that?"

She lifted a shoulder as she raised the loosened tie over his head and dropped it over her own. A flip of a couple of buttons and she lowered to sit on her feet.

"I must agree. It looks much better on you."

"If you lose the coat, I'll fix your sleeves."

Ellis hesitated as if he were considering her offer. Finally, he straightened and pulled it from his shoulders. One at a time, he held out his arms, allowing her to roll them up.

"Ready for a stroll?" he asked, moving to his feet.

Arabella stood and began gathering the lunch remnants to drop into the trash bin as they passed. Ellis carefully folded his suit jacket and placed it into the bag she'd brought with them. She dug for her sunglasses and plopped the floppy hat onto her head. With a grin, she pulled the ballcap from underneath his jacket and waved at him.

"That seems a bit excessive." Ellis gained his footing and scooped up everything.

With his arms occupied, Arabella took advantage and hopped, slapping the cap onto his head. "We can't have your head get sunburned."

Ellis ducked his head, casting her a look that she felt trickle down her spine. "Princess, you do realize the path you are treading, don't you?"

That trickle landed in her stomach, swirling and mocking her. His nonresistance now required her nonresistance later. "Not sucking your dick." She whirled, scooping up her shoes as she turned. She had never witnessed a laugh from him, but if asked, she would swear he just did. Her back stiff, she set out walking toward the caboose. She decided to call it a cough mixed with the squeal of kids' laughter and not look back.

The occasional breeze eased the heat of the rays beaming down as they walked side by side in silence. Recently cut blades of grass pricked the bottoms of her feet. She pushed the sunglasses further up her nose and hurried across the blacktop on her toes cringing at the burn. "A gentleman would have carried me across the heated road," she shot over her shoulder without a glance his way.

"A lady would have paused to slip on her shoes, giving the gentleman a chance to whisk her off her feet."

"Guess I'm no lady then."

"And I'm far from a gentleman."

Arabella jerked to a stop, throwing her hands to her hips. "Hold on. You didn't even flinch. You agree I'm not a lady?"

"Princess, I flinch for nothing, and you are the perfect woman." He peered down to where she stood with her arms now crossed. "And we are perfect together. A perfect fit." He moved a step closer. "In all the right places."

Arabella's chin dropped. When would she learn? She had no words jump to mind, so she spun and set out toward the pond again.

Shimmers of white light rippled over the water, flashing through the thick, dark lenses she wore. The chatter of a nearby squirrel caught her attention. She slowed and searched the treetops. Ellis said nothing but slipped the straps of her shoes from her fingers and placed the breadcrumbs in her hand.

His phone buzzed, pausing any conversation between the two. With a glance he told her, "I must take this. Take your time." He answered it as he moved toward the staggered layers of ground used for seating during outdoor performances. "Not possible to meet today. Tomorrow morning, ten o'clock at the . . ." And his voice faded.

Arabella smiled, knowing he delayed business to spend the day with her. She pinpointed the fowl and set off to feed them. For the next while, she became lost in the serenity of the surrounding nature. So peaceful. Eventually, she strolled back to where Ellis sat and settled beside him. "Have you enjoyed any of this?"

"I'm enjoying the view immensely." He held his phone in front of her.

She glanced down and her heart lifted. There on the screen, she was offering a treat to one of the ducks. "I love that."

"I understand you terminated your phone to cut costs. Is that correct?"

Arabella nodded. It seemed like a large sacrifice at the time, but in reality, she hadn't missed it much at all. Although there had been times in the past few weeks she wanted to reach out to her father. But Ellis did have a landline in the kitchen she had used.

He lifted her foot onto his lap and slipped a shoe on, working the tiny buckle. "Gus will be here soon. We'll have you one in no time."

"Really?"

He replaced her foot with the other and reached for the remaining shoe. "Of course."

"Can I take a photo with yours until I get one?"

He slipped the strap underneath the narrow metal tab, placed her foot to the ground, and reached again for his phone. Without a word, he handed it over.

Arabella wasted no time for him to change his mind or give an argument. She pulled up the camera and leaned close to Ellis. The instant his eyes appeared on the screen, she snapped the memory. "Thank you."

He said nothing but gazed down locking eyes with her, preventing her from moving away. The back of his finger grazed her cheek, numbing her thoughts. The heat of his palm sliding behind her neck paralyzed her until the tug of his fingers twisting in her hair brought a gasp from her. He closed in, capturing her mouth and taking control of her thoughts. She could feel her chest rising, forcing air into her lungs as the sounds of nature faded away. She leaned into him, devouring the taste of his kiss.

Suddenly, she felt the loss of him and searched his eyes. Staring back at her, they darkened and left her aching for more.

"That's for us." His voice came across low and heavy.

"What?" she whispered as the car horn blasted again.

"That. Gus is getting impatient. Or rather he thinks I've turned deaf."

Arabella jerked her head toward the sound. The beating of her heart had drowned out the horn. Heat filled her chest, threatening to rise into her cheeks.

"We shall continue this later," he promised.

***

Arabella leaned into Ellis's side and stared into the darkness beyond the window. The tinted glass emphasized the night sky, giving only a hint of the streetlights rolling past. The day had been wonderful. A surprising treat that restored a feeling of normalcy to her life. And although he had announced that he was no gentleman, which she'd already known, he portrayed the perfect gentleman all evening.

Her hand snaked down, touching her small purse next to her. It held the cell phone she now had. Her connection to the outside world, as Ellis had put it. It was a thoughtful gift, one she appreciated greatly, and felt it was more of a sacrifice for Ellis to relinquish that bit of control than he let on. She'd known he was controlling, but until moving in, she had no idea of the extent. The phone was like adding a few inches to her leash while adding another venue of power. He had his number along with her father's number programed into it. It didn't matter how he viewed the gift, she thought it a lovely gesture.

His hand fell to her knee, bringing her attention back to him. She glanced up, studying his profile. His expression revealed nothing as he surveyed the darkness. She wondered what was going through his mind. Business? Their evening? Her? Did any of it really matter? She decided that, no, it didn't. He had taken her to a five-star restaurant for an intimate dinner. It was a bit of a drive, but well worth it. The food was scrumptious, and their private table set the mood for a romantic evening. She highly doubted that was his intention, but she loved it anyway. Other than one phone call that he insisted was necessary to take and walked away, the evening had been perfect.

Soon, they were traveling up the drive to the house, and Ellis turned, flashing her a smile.

She returned his smile and gathered her purse, slipping her wrist through the small, looped opening. The moment the SUV stopped, they climbed out and Ellis wrapped his hand around hers, then gathered the bag of things they'd collected throughout the day with the other. A swift shove to the door with his elbow sent it swinging closed. He leaned toward the passenger window sliding open. "That's all for now. Remain alert until further notice."

A mumble of words drifted from the vehicle, although Arabella could not hear them clearly, before Ellis gave a final nod and led them to the door.

Inside, Arabella paused on the bottom step, leaving Ellis on the floor and bringing them to an equal height. Eye to eye, she relieved him of the bag hanging from his fingers. "Today was amazing. Thank you." She lifted her hand to his shoulder and leaned forward. Quick as a flash, her lips warmed his. Then, just as fast, she spun away, running up the steps.

"Go shower."

His words caught her off guard and she nearly stumbled, jerking to a halt and planting both feet on one step as she twisted toward him. "I'm not—"

His glare and raised brow interrupted her rejection. "Go. Shower."

Her heart began to race, and her lips parted. But no words came as she was met with a more intense glare trumping her determination. She whirled and ran up the last few steps and into her room. She slammed the door shut and fell against it. Her heart was in a marathon now, and her mouth became a desert. Not to mention the thousands of butterflies that had just made their way into her stomach. All from one look. All from two words. Damn that book.

Arabella dropped the large bag from the park next to her feet and tossed her purse onto the bed. Within seconds, she sat on the edge of the tub. Catching her breath, it dawned on her that she hadn't taken the time to select her night clothes from the bureau to bring in here. Her shoulders drooped and she tossed back her head. The day had been so perfect, then in one look, she was a hot mess.

She took a deep breath and straightened. Her eyes popped open and there in front of her was her robe. She smiled. How could she forget that she'd left it in here in case Ellis barged in on her again. A laugh bubbled up inside and erupted only to be silenced by a tap on the door.

"I'm placing an ice bucket on the balcony for you. Do you have a preference of its contents?"

"None, thank you," she called back without a thought.

"I'll be in my office for a while if you should need me."

His office? Her entire body felt as if the rubber band winding around it had snapped and relieved all the tension. He had been the perfect date all evening, she reminded herself. Just as he had informed her earlier in the day, today was her "thank you" treat. Her choice. He knew she would not choose sex. Besides, business first.

Falling back into her happy fairytale mood, she hopped to her feet, undressed, and stepped into the shower. With the temperature to her liking, she engaged each set of waterheads. Every muscle in her body slumped and her eyelids slid closed. The constant drum of water tapped against her skin from all directions as if she were standing naked in a rainforest during a storm. Warm water cascaded down her body, removing all inhibitions she'd conjured up about the evening's end. Fully refreshed, and before wrinkles began to alter her fingertips, she made quick work of the shampoo and conditioner before stepping out and towel drying her hair. With slow and languid movements, she reached for the robe that she'd fallen in love with, pulling the lapels tight to her neck, breathing in the clean scent and savoring the softness. She looped the sash into a bow that dangled in a comfortable spot, then made her way to the balcony.

The night air was rejuvenating. A slight breeze brushed her skin. She turned toward the chair's position between the two sets of doors leading to the bedrooms, hers and Ellis's. As promised, a bucket sat on the small table chilling a long slender bottle with a wine glass next to it. Draped over the arm of the nearest seat was her quilt that she'd brought with her. She couldn't deny the peacefulness filling her nor could she fight the smile taking over.

Settling in and wrapping the worn quilt over her legs, she filled the goblet and leaned back, becoming lost in the serenade of crickets rising from below accompanied by a rustle of leaves in the distance. A lone bird called out occasionally, searching for its mate. She savored another sip of the sweet watermelon wine noting a whippoorwill beginning its nightly concert. It had been so long since she'd had the leisure of sitting and listening to the sounds of the night.

One glass down, she filled another, leaving it to rest next to the ice bucket as she repositioned the quilt. A little cushion over the metal seat wouldn't hurt. She settled onto the end of the material and flipped the opposite end over her lap, more for comfort than for warmth. The slickness of the robe slid from her knee hanging over the other with the movement of the quilt. The night air kissing her legs sent a shiver through her. She swirled another taste of wine around her mouth, letting it trickle down her throat before reaching to cover them.

"Leave it."

Arabella swung her head toward Ellis emerging from his room. Dressed in nothing more than boxer briefs and a shirt that hung open, he walked to the balustrade and relaxed his ass against it. Muscles flexed in his legs as he lifted one ankle across the other and swirled the ice in his tumbler after a sip. The glass tinked against the metal as he held it in place, keeping it from teetering to either the ground or the floor. Her gaze followed his free hand as it ran over his beard, smoothing any wild strays into place. It had lengthened some since her arrival. Gray that still held a touch of bright ginger near the sides had the magic to send shivers through her each time he leaned close to touch a nerve.

"You're staring."

Caught, Arabella forced her focus to the blue staring back at her. "You're not dressed."

"That tends to happen after a shower." His eyes roamed her with a quirk of his lips. "I venture to say you have less on than I do."

She lifted her drink. "That tends to happen when I'm relaxing with a bottle of wine."

"Then drink up." Ellis lifted his glass toward hers, then downed a large portion of its contents.

"Are you trying to get me drunk?"

"If I wanted you drunk, I would have given you something stronger."

"So, you just want me naked?"

"I know how to do that without alcohol."

No denying that. He'd learned to work her like a puppet. Or maybe she had simply fallen under his spell. She lifted the glass to her lips, taking in the sight of him, from the light curls blending in with his chest down to his feet.

"You're staring again."

The glass landed on the metal with a thud when Arabella stood. "I can't be accused of staring from my bed. Good night."

Ellis lunged from his spot, reaching out and grabbing Arabella, tugging her until she crashed into his chest. The tie holding her robe closed cut into her waist from his fingers twisting in it, holding her hostage. Air whooshed from her on impact, parting her lips and allowing his tongue to invade. A dizziness fluttered through her, chasing away what little reason she had. Her fingers grasped for stability, digging into his sides.

The kiss was brash and hungry. He tasted of whisky, dark and dangerous. Yes, he was dangerous, and she was powerless against his kiss, his touch, his will.

Long, devouring kisses melted Arabella. Her fingers released their death grip on his sides and snaked inside his shirt. Smooth and uneven ripples up his back warmed her touch. Or maybe it was the heat growing in her that warmed him. She couldn't be certain. Her mind had blurred, not realizing when they had moved. Nor when the ties fell to her sides. His eyes held her captive as he straightened. The thud of his tumbler against the table echoed through the darkness. She pressed her hand into his back.

His nostrils flared, and with a jerk of her robe, her hands fell from the warmth of him. Her arms now bound to her sides by her own clothing, she was helpless to move. A flash of evil and satisfaction passed through his eyes, and she found herself cradled in the cushion of her quilt as he jerked the sash from her waist. "Grip the chair," he growled and began winding the sash around her wrists, binding her to the seat. She was fully exposed, with the robe restricting her arm movements further by being twisted behind her. Ellis's movements were too quick for her to process until he paused to appreciate his work. No, he was examining his work. He was studying her like an eagle zeroes in on his prey before swooping in for the kill. He was silent, calculating. Adrenaline rushed through her, attacking her chest and seizing her breath. The corner of his lips twitched. "Breathe."

She sucked in a gasp of air letting it flow out.

"Good girl. Now close your eyes."

Arabella's eyelids drifted closed as if she had no control over them. The caress of fingers on her cheek ignited chills that shot through her when he closed them around her neck, nudging it back onto the chair. Her heartbeat nearly drowned out his voice.

"Just feel."

"I need to feel you," she whispered.

"Oh, princess, you're gonna feel me. Here." His fingers tightened, stopping a fraction before he took her breath and trailed down her throat. "Here." Both hands warmed her breasts, tweaking her already tightening nipples. "Then here." The night air kissed her nipples, cooling them after losing the heat of his touch only to heighten her desire. Firm massages over her stomach and down each leg transported her into a euphoria she was unable to fight. But then, she had no desire to fight it. Ellis manipulated her body like a charm, touching and teasing every inch. Every inch other than where she ached to be touched.

"Ellis," she moaned, eyes still hidden.

"Yes?"

Before she formed her thought, let alone respond, his tongue swirled over an areola. Her chest lifted, searching for more until it puckered, tightening, molding to his mouth. Still, he teased, torturing her core. Working every nerve in her body but one—that one begging for attention.

"Are you ready to pay up on our little wager?"

She could feel his breath against her skin, the thick tickle of facial hair pausing her answer while shivers exploded like fireworks in her body. His thigh pressed against her folds, and he leaned over her.

"Did someone just come?"

Arabella's head moved in a shiver more than a shake. "No," she breathed.

"No, you're not ready to pay up? Because you can't lie about what's running down my leg."

Her scalp prickled from the strands twisting tighter in his fingers.

"Open your eyes."

She gripped the metal as her body lurched upright, finding herself awkwardly perched on the edge of the seat. His leg still pressed against the dampness between her legs, holding her on the edge of the chair and the edge of release. She stared at the raging arousal inches from her face.

"Are we paying up or walking away?"

She shot a glare upward best she could manage with her hair wound so tightly in his fingers. Every dirty word she knew ran through her mind and silently flew from her tongue when it darted toward him. She hooked a leg around his, begging him to remain close. Slow and steady, she tasted the length of the engorged flesh teasing the ridge. "I can't." She flicked her tongue. "Can't reach."

"Need help?"

Arabella's head bounced, tightening her grip on his leg as she became mesmerized by the sight of his hand sliding around the base of his dick, positioning himself for her. Her lips slipped over him, sliding down the shaft with his hand pushing her to her limit. He pulled her back, then pushed again. His hand fell away, relieving the tension on her scalp and she continued the rhythm. Sucking, swirling, licking. Her eyelids drifted closed again as she focused on thoroughly exploring every vein and inch of the smooth steel of his cock.

"Damn, woman," Ellis bit out between clenched teeth. He pulled from her mouth and fell to his knees, jerking her forward and leaving her teetering on the edge.

She gasped, the metal of the chair arm cutting into her palms. Her knees fell wide with a shove from Ellis, and he thrust inside her. Her sudden scream filled the night, and he froze. Her wide eyes darted to meet his then dropped to the tightness of his jaw and veins bulging in his neck. A moment's hesitation and his arm wrapped her body, behind her back, and fingers dug into her flesh. He slammed the opposite hand onto the seat next to her butt, all gentleness from the day gone as he furiously pumped in and out of her, carrying them both to the edge.

Arabella floated higher and higher until the instant his tongue darted out, flicking her nipple once more. Her body spasmed and she jerked upward toward Ellis, her teeth digging into his shoulder. His cock pulsating inside her, warm cum filled her as another orgasm shattered through her body.

She fell limp, however awkwardly, as her shoulder blades pinched together, leaving her bound wrists above her head. Relief shot through her arms as soon as Ellis pulled the sash, letting it drop to the floor. He rocked back to lean against the railing with Arabella on his lap. Neither spoke a word as the coolness swirled around them and the whippoorwill song filled the air once again.

Kiss of Power

Jewelz Baxter

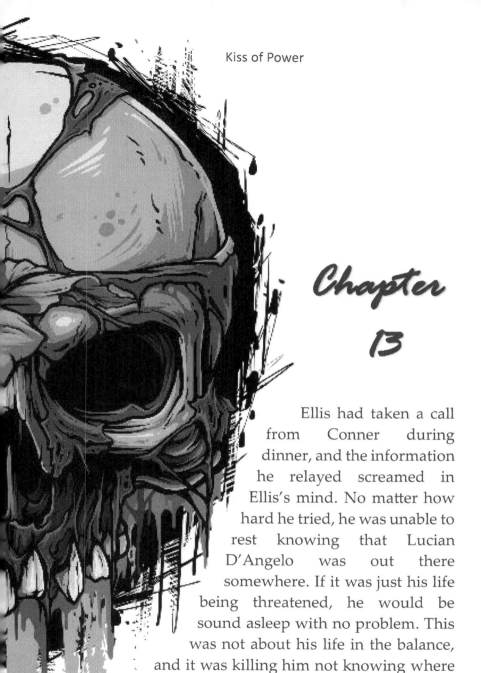

Chapter 13

Ellis had taken a call from Conner during dinner, and the information he relayed screamed in Ellis's mind. No matter how hard he tried, he was unable to rest knowing that Lucian D'Angelo was out there somewhere. If it was just his life being threatened, he would be sound asleep with no problem. This was not about his life in the balance, and it was killing him not knowing where the predator was lying in wait. Sleep eluded him. Even forcing his eyes to close only brought images he knew he must prevent. Adrenaline thrummed through his body, propelling him from room to room. He'd made phone calls all evening, and now, he paced the floors.

He jerked the phone from the wall in the kitchen and dialed.

"What's going on?" he barked the moment Conner answered.

"It's not good. We located his car. It was wrecked and abandoned about sixty-five miles from here. Alex should be there at sun-up to gather all he can."

"Any idea on the timeframe?"

"None yet. It's a wait and see game now. He may not even be headed this way."

"He's here. I feel it."

"That may be. Have you gotten any sleep? It's four a.m."

"I can't sleep until that son of a bitch is taken out."

"Ellis, we've dealt with his kind before."

"This is different. I can take it without blinking an eye, but I can't lay that fear on someone one else."

"That's not true. Anyone else you wouldn't give a shit. You care about Arabella, and the quicker you admit it, the lighter you'll feel. Stop lying to yourself. Go crawl into bed with her and get some sleep."

"Not happening."

"Then keep pacing and I'll sleep so I can cover your ass tomorrow."

"I'll inform Bartel, Tucker, and Dawson."

"If Bartel knows, he may tip his hand," Conner pointed out.

"Yeah, you're right."

"I'm going to sleep."

Ellis hooked the receiver back onto the base and moved to the window. The moon spread across the still waters of the pool, illuminating the veranda. The clear night showcased the scene in a haze like an outdated snapshot. Silent with no movement.

One more walkthrough and he'd make his way upstairs. He'd already stood at her door, silently leaning against the wall, watching her sleep.

He straightened and moved toward the formal dining room when a slight creak stopped him in his tracks. Hairs on his neck prickled. He slipped his weapon from its holster and eased toward the sound. A faint shadow passed the entrance floor. So slight that if he had not been pacing the darkness for hours, he most likely would not have noticed it. He pressed a shoulder to the wall. Seconds felt like minutes as he waited. Anger filled him, growing into rage at the idea of someone threatening Arabella.

The gun would wake her. Knock him out and drag him outside, he decided. He quickly returned the gun to its place. She needn't see evidence when she awoke. A form stepped through the door, shrouded in the darkness. He whirled, one hand circling the small neck, squeezing, shoving the intruder against the wall while the other raised and coming down hard. Arabella screamed, cutting through his rage, but he was in full swing. His fist landed next to her head with a force he was unable to stop. His chest heaved, rendering him motionless as he looked into her eyes. Her chest rose in rhythm with his, brushing his arm with each gasp for air. Her fingers dug into his wrist still pressing her against the wall. He pulled his fist from the wall and his shoulders dropped. One by one, his fingers loosened, allowing air back into her lungs.

He didn't move as she rubbed her neck. He could have killed her. If he had not been aware of keeping the deed from her, his Glock would have pressed against her temple ripping away his heart.

"What are you doing up?" Ellis growled.

She coughed and forced a swallow. "I wanted a drink of water."

Water. His jaw ticked from the pressure, and he whirled toward the refrigerator. He slung open the door grabbing a bottle from the door and shoved it closed. "Water. Take it with you." He realized the harshness of his voice. But it was better than the alternative. He shoved it into her hand.

"Are you alright?" She hadn't moved from the wall. She fumbled with the bottle, watching him.

"I'm fine. Go to bed."

She stepped closer.

"I said go to bed." His bark bit him as much as it did her.

She spun on the spot and ran from him and up the stairs, disappearing in her room. But not quick enough for him to miss the glint from her tear-filled eyes.

He rolled his head toward the hole left of his fist. He'd never once been this reckless. Conner was right, he had to make changes. He searched out the time. Almost five. He moved back to the phone and made two of the three original calls he had earlier planned, both quick and precise. His focus fell back onto the wall damage as he passed. He should have it patched first thing, but no, not yet. More important things were at hand. Plus, it would serve as a reminder of what he must do.

Exhaustion reared its head and weighed his steps like lead, slowing his ascent to the bedrooms. His door made no sound as he entered. He moved straight through the connecting doors to her bed. He stood over her, not sure whether he wished for her to be awake or asleep. She made no sound, no movement. He pulled the large chair near her bed as quietly as possible and settle in. Slouched with his elbow on the arm, he dropped his head in his hand and kicked his feet onto the edge of the mattress. Within seconds, sleep at last settled in.

***

The next day, Arabella hopped down the stairs, pivoting toward the rear of the house. Bypassing the kitchen and breakfast, she swung open the veranda door and focused on the grove of trees where she was headed.

"Arabella."

She rolled to a halt, staring straight ahead and stiffening her back. Her brain screamed to run before he could order her to turn around. "Good morning, Ellis." Slowly, she gained another step.

"Arabella."

She froze. Arabella. Not Princess. This couldn't be good.

His voice pierced the silence once more, harsh and demanding. "Come have a seat."

On a sigh, she spun toward him, moving to the table he occupied.

"Would you like something from the kitchen?"

"No, thank you." She eased into the chair next to him. "I figured you would be couped up in your office already."

"Did you sleep well?"

"I did, thank you. Although, I doubt you did, cramped in that chair."

He lifted his mug to his lips, giving no indication one way or another of his feelings on sleeping in her room. Taking his time returning the coffee to the table, he raised his gaze to hers. "A couple of things."

"Okay, shoot."

"You felt my back."

His voice had taken on an unfamiliar tone, sending a flock of butterflies to her stomach.

"As you know now, I am indeed the boss of the Darby family. That includes all aspects of the business. A blessing or a curse, it is who I am."

Arabella remained motionless as he paused and only gave a slight nod when his eyes met hers again.

"What you felt is the results of my instruction. My branding, one might say. I do not apologize for who or what I am. I have, however, made a point not to repulse you with those certain facts."

"You were beaten?"

"Whipped. Lashings were thought to instill a permanent reminder of the lessons. I learned quickly to retain every word spoken and act on every deed commanded.

"That's horrible."

"That's life. Now, only three people know of this, of my scars."

"You and your brothers?"

"You and me. The third is dead."

Arabella felt her eyes widen and forced them away to control them. "Conner and Alex don't know?"

"Not the extent."

She lifted her gaze back to Ellis, and he leaned forward, folding his arms onto the edge of the table.

"No one, and I mean *no one*, else is to be privileged to this fact."

"I promise."

His nod was quick but reassuring that they had reached an agreement. She wondered if this was how his customers felt. A mixture of fear and awe. Not really fear, at least not for her, but she did understand the possible threat he just issued.

"How's your neck?"

Her fingers flew to the edge of her shirt, lightly touching the tenderness.

He reached out, brushing away her hand and tugging the material lower. "I noticed the bruise when you stepped outside."

"It's a bit tender, but it will fade."

"Now, what's the question filling those eyes?"

"Would you have really walked away last night?"

Arabella watched the glimmer sneak back in, brightening the blue of his eyes. "Any other person would be taken aback by my ultimatum, or the fact I could have killed you last night, and here you are asking about sex."

"Good thing I'm not just anyone else. I won't betray you, and you won't hurt me. We both know that." She dropped her head to the side. "So, would you have?"

"Would you have really not tasted the very thing you now crave?"

Arabella fell to the backrest of the seat and crossed her arms. "You're so full of it. I never said I crave you. Or . . ." She waved a hand and gave a nod toward his crotch. "Him."

His lips twisted into a lopsided grin. "Well, I know the truth, and he thanks you."

Arabella rolled her eyes. She tugged her sleeve back over her wrist and tucked her hands against her sides. "Here's another truth you should know. I'm not repulsed by any scars on your back or any other place you've been concealing them. I hate that happened to you, but it's just a superficial thing that doesn't change the way I see you." She paused, but no response or rebuttal came. Speechless. She couldn't say she had witnessed him speechless before.

With a playful grin, she stood, bumping the chair back with her legs. "Now, this princess is off to check on her baby. That is, if you are amenable, master."

Ellis huffed on a smile and waved her away.

Jewelz Baxter

Chapter 14

A week's time had passed since the dinner party, and the exchange of favors had altered their relationship, so to speak. Arabella had conceded they were on their way to becoming friends, and Ellis scoffed, reminding her that the friend zone had been thrown to the wayside long ago. Either way, the bickering remained and the discipline escalated. Which also brought a new set of boundaries, including freedoms that

Arabella negotiated. Today was one of those negotiated times.

Sandals in hand, Arabella walked through the grass to the swing in her father's yard. The air was warm from the sun, and wildflowers were beginning to bloom alongside the road. Arabella pointed her toe into the grass, pushing the swing into motion. She threw back her head, soaking in the fading sun. Her phone rang next to her leg, and without looking, she lifted it, touching the spot she knew would bring Ellis's voice to life. She'd been so excited when he surprised her with the device. It was glued to her side anytime she was away from him. Of course, she complained and ranted when he reminded her to carry it, but inside, she smiled, even though she talked to no one but Ellis and her father. Twice she had reached out to a friend from the time she'd lived in Dallas.

"Hey you."

"Have you had a good visit?"

She smiled. "I have. Burger King and I shared a full bag of marshmallows."

"I refuse to swap cow spittle."

Arabella burst into laughter. "You do have limits. I'll be sure to visit with a treat every day. Nothing else has kept you off me."

"I never said I'd keep my hands from you. I'll shower you first."

She jumped to her feet. "I made dinner and packed a dish for us. Let me run inside and grab it."

"I can get that for you when I get there. You know I'll speak to your father before we head home."

"Funny. Sit still, I'll only be a moment. Papa had a neighbor call. A cow got out and they're corralling him back in and fixing the break."

"You're alone?"

"I'm a big girl." She stepped back into the evening air. "Thanks for opening the door, I guess. But the back seat? And I thought you were in your car."

"I am in the car. Who's there?"

"Don't test me. I know the details of your vehicles." She wedged the phone onto her shoulder, leaning her cheek onto it. "There." She slid the dish on the floorboard.

"No!" His voice was faint as her cheek muffled the speaker when she climbed into the SUV. She pulled the door closed and straightened.

His voice faded as the phone tumbled to the floor.

"Don't get in! Don't hang up!"

She lunged toward the door and jerked the handle.

A chilling laugh wrapped around her. "Child locks. Keeps the child in and keeps the monsters away."

She fell against the seat as the SUV charged through the yard and launched from the ditch onto the road, tossing her like a rag doll on the seat. "Who are you?"

"Your avenging angel. You people think you're so high and mighty because you inherit land. While others struggle to own a house, you roam acres and acres of ground that should belong to those struggling to live."

Arabella's fingers tightened on the edge of the seat, the phone forgotten on the floor and the dish of food bouncing around her feet along with her shoes. She stared ahead, trying to spot a familiar landmark. The darkness hid their direction, but they had to be traveling away from town and any streetlights. The doors were locked, so no chance of her jumping if they slowed. Dread sunk in. No one knew where she was. She didn't even know where she was or where they were headed.

"What do you want? Where are you taking me?"

"Somewhere to get acquainted while we wait for dear old dad to give me what I deserve."

"He'll never move from that farm."

"I don't plan for him to leave it. I'll bury him right next to you. I'm thinking in a pasture where your animals can take a shit on you every day until they die along with you. I'll build one house after another until there's not an inch left."

"You can build a housing complex anywhere," Arabella shouted, still clutching the seat.

"Oh, but then I'll move past your precious farm and move into that mansion and surround it with houses. Houses of people devoted to me. I'll be more powerful than that waste of breath you like to fuck."

Who is this man? She strained to see his face. Between the darkness and the ballcap pulled low, his identity remained a mystery. His voice triggered no memory either. But she refused to give him the satisfaction of seeing fear. She leaned, jerking at the door again. It failed, and she tried the other door.

Her stomach churned from the sound of his laughter. "I'm going to be sick."

"I don't care. Not my ride. Puke everywhere."

She dropped her forehead to the back of the driver's seat. Her heart threatened to jump from her chest, and she squeezed her eyes. Sweat beaded across her forehead. Her body lurched slightly, and she sucked in a deep breath before wrapping her arm around the seat and his head. The bill of the cap dug into her arm. His curses fell silent, drowned out by the pounding in her own head. Air whooshed from her lungs as her body was launched and wedged between the front bucket seats. Her hand shot to the steering wheel, pulling with all her strength. Her body flailed away from the assailant and the world slowed. Her back curled around the passenger seat, throwing her legs into the driver's seat. The smooth road had disappeared and the SUV plunged, tossing her into the dash. The rough descent was short but steep, halting with a jerk.

Arabella landed half on the seat and half on the floor and opened her eyes. She jerked toward the man slumped over the steering wheel. No movement. She could waste no time. She climbed onto the seat and pushed open the door an inch or so, but then it refused to budge. Water began leaking in through the crack it had created. The window. Yes! It opened and she pulled herself onto the door.

Cold fingers wrapped around her ankle. "Not so fast, bitch."

She refused to fall back onto the seat. She kicked frantically, and her fingers grew numb around the metal doorframe. She was not going out like this. Not on an unknown road with a stranger. "No!" Her scream echoed through the falling darkness as she shoved her heel into his face and fell to the ground.

It was a short distance, and the thick mud underneath a hand's width of water softened her fall. She struggled to her feet and began trudging up the embankment. Her mud-covered feet slid over the grass as she dug her fingers and toes into the earth in an effort to resist the sliding. The night air amplified the sounds around her, and light flashed above her. A car. She screamed until the sound of wheels along the blacktop faded past. Her assailant's voice mocked her. He was alive and the stab of his voice sent her heart straight into her throat. She reached a trembling hand toward the base of a sapling just above her.

A faint roar met her ears, and she began screaming again. This car had to hear her. She was near the top of the slope. What if they didn't hear her? What if they heard but kept driving? What if it wasn't a car? What if the building roar was the fear thrumming through her body? "Nooo!" Her throat burned from the force of her voice.

Finally, she managed to work herself to get a foothold on the sapling. His voice grew louder. Closer. She could hear him, but his words had become a backdrop for the pounding in her ears. A faint glow began to grow above her, and she scrambled to reach for it. Hairs prickled her spine as her fingers touched the dry gravel that lined the road. An icy coldness wrapped her, pulling her backward. She swung her free leg, flipping onto her back, then struck out at him and grasping at the ground around her.

"You're going to pay for that." The man sounded like the devil himself standing above her. His grip tightened, digging into her leg as he stared down at her. His shoulders lifted with each gasp for air, his breath a raspy growl reminding her of a rabid animal calculating his strike.

A light appeared out of nowhere, like a stagehand placing him into the spotlight. His head jerked up, revealing his face for the first time with his eyes squinting into the beam.

"Help me!"

"I'm here, Princess."

Could she believe her ears? Princess? "Ellis!"

"D'Angelo!" Ellis shouted from the edge of the road.

Lucian dropped her leg, inching toward Ellis. "Well, well, now. Look a here. Two for one. I didn't expect to get a shot at you this soon."

"You best take your shot now. When I reach you, you die."

Arabella listened to Ellis's voice grow closer but kept her focus on her kidnapper.

He reached behind him, and Arabella rolled into his legs, knocking him off balance. A thud echoed next to her head, and she flinched. She jerked toward the gun, stretching to retrieve it before the assailant. The tip of her fingers grazed the metal, and two strong hands pulled her from its reach. "Stay back." Ellis's words blanketed her fear. She rose onto her palms, inching away. Ellis turned and Lucian's fist caught him, tossing his head to the side. Ellis swung, connecting with a similar punch to Lucian's cheek. Lucian stumbled and his head wobbled. Ellis grabbed his shirt, twisting his hand into the material and reaching under his suit coat.

The glint cast by the car headlights onto the Glock drew Arabella's focus until Ellis shoved the barrel into the man's throat. She jerked away, squeezing her eyes, waiting for the intense silence that had fallen to shatter. Her hands muffled the blast. Fear and relief warred inside, delaying the moment she turned back toward Ellis. His pistol was back in its place, and he held a handkerchief, wiping evidence from his face and hands. He stuffed the red-stained cloth into a pocket and turned toward her.

In two steps, he was next to her, and she was in his arms. She clung to him as he managed the incline. Glancing back over his shoulder, any doubt Lucian D'Angelo would return disappeared. He laid with dead eyes staring into the night, crimson spilling into the muddy debris around him.

Ellis placed her into his passenger seat and stretched the seatbelt over her. He hurried around the car and wasted no time driving them home. The drive was silent. Although no words passed between them, the constant contact of his hand around hers spoke volumes to Arabella. Maybe he wasn't the monster she'd accused him of being.

Kiss of Power

Jewelz Baxter

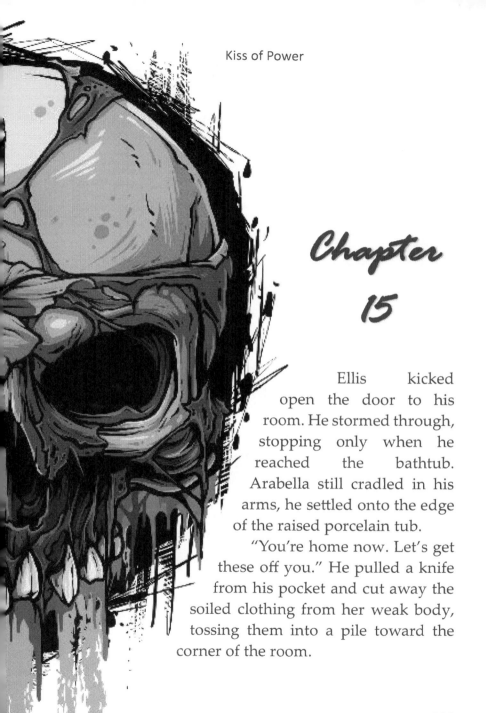

Chapter 15

Ellis kicked open the door to his room. He stormed through, stopping only when he reached the bathtub. Arabella still cradled in his arms, he settled onto the edge of the raised porcelain tub.

"You're home now. Let's get these off you." He pulled a knife from his pocket and cut away the soiled clothing from her weak body, tossing them into a pile toward the corner of the room.

Her arm snapped around his neck, pressing her body against his. The way she clung to him was like a bullet killing all his inhibitions. Not that he was self-conscious. He'd always been taught not to feel, that emotions had no place in life. Especially if you wanted to be somebody. You need to remain in control, and emotions were only a loss of control.

The thought of losing Arabella had been suffocating him. He had feared for her death during the struggle. Then the thought of her growing cold from fear of him cut deep. But if he had ever questioned her feelings, now was definitely not one of those times. Nothing but trust and security could bring her to trust him this way. And love.

He pressed his lips to the top of her head and gave way to the smile spurred by her squeeze, however slight, against his neck. "Let's get you cleaned up."

He twisted the knobs and adjusted the water temperature, remaining intently aware of her being fully exposed and clinging to him. His arm tightened as he splayed his fingers over her back. He focused on the level of the water, twisting the knobs once again to bring it to a stop. He stood, lifting her, and turned, dropping a knee to the raised floor and easing her into the water. Pushing to his feet, his gaze never left her, even as the buttons from his shirt flew across the room.

He ripped it from his shoulders and tossed it onto the disposed clothing, then he dropped back to his knees. "Ellis."

Her cheek was warm in his palm. Slowly, her fingertip traced from the corner of his eye down his cheek. "You're hurt."

He couldn't deny the smile tugging his lips. He caught her hand and placed a kiss to her wrist. "It's just a scratch."

Ellis stretched for the soap. "Lie back and relax. Let me take care of you."

She tilted her head back, her neck fitting the curve of the tub perfectly. A slight twitch of her still red lips was not lost on him. Lips he wanted on him, though this was not about him. This was about her, as much of his life had become. Her eyelids drifted close, and he lathered his hands. He began with her hands and up her arms, taking away the evidence of her struggles. At least the surface evidence, the mud and the blood spatters. No doubt bruises would appear by morning. He cringed inside, realizing the pain she must be in.

Ellis spread the lather over her curves and her firmness. Taking his time and paying great attention to the delicate areas. Tiny movements of her cheeks alerted him to these sensations each touch of his fingertips brought and each time his palm smoothed across her softness.

Scooping handfuls of water, he rinsed away the suds. Abandoning her for only a moment, he moved to a cabinet filled with her personal items. Searching a collection of bottles and tubes, he decided on a large tube labeled cleanser and a tube resembling lipstick that was labeled remover. He grabbed two fresh cloths as he passed the shelf and knelt back where he was before.

He squeezed a small amount of white lotion into his hand. "Keep your eyes closed." He began slow, expecting a flinch the moment his fingertips touched her face. But there was none. Not even when he soaked the cloth and cleansed away what was left of her makeup along with the last of the reminders of her encounter.

He retrieved the small tube and gently applied it over the deep red. Then with the last cloth, the red disappeared. He surrendered to the pull of her innocence and pure beauty. His thumb glided across her bottom lip. This is how he liked her best, stripped of all superficial grandeur and fear. He loved the simpleness of her beauty and how it radiated through her.

And her innocence. His lips lifted as he traced hers once more. She thought she knew the monster that filled him, but the true depth of his evil she had not witnessed. And he vowed she never would. His true being he kept hidden from her. She needed to see only the kind side that she'd brought to life.

He flipped a switch, sending the water away. "Time to dry off." He scooped her from the water still swirling lower and lower and placed her on her feet. "I'm sure you'll be sore tomorrow. I'll get you something to help you relax." He jerked a towel from a stack next to the tub and began dabbing away the beads of water.

"Why—"

Her words fell away with a gentle kiss. "Don't fret over it tonight. Or give it a second thought. You're safe. Just know I'll protect you no matter the cost."

"But you—"

Again, he stopped her words. "I'm unharmed. Just a bit disheveled. You rest, and we'll discuss this later if we must."

Arabella surrendered with a nod.

He dried his arms and chest, then lifted her once again. Her softness warmed his chest and her head rested on his shoulder as he carried her to his bed. Once she was settled, he returned to the bathroom for a glass of water and pain medication. He placed them both in her hands and combed the damp hair from her face. "Take these and rest. I'm going to shower, and I'll be back."

He waited the few seconds it took for her to swallow the pills, then he took the glass, carrying it back to the bathroom with him. He slid it onto the lavatory and studied himself in the mirror. His suit was ruined, not that he cared. And he had never cared who saw the results of any action he felt led to take. But the thought of Arabella witnessing it, viewing the blood-soaked ground and stained clothing, stung his pride. It was his job to shield her from these things, to never allow her the privilege of meeting the true monster she believed he was. The monster he knew he'd been trained to be. He closed his eyes on a deep breath reminding himself he only did what was needed.

He removed his shoes and his pants, adding them to the pile in the corner. He snaked his hand into a cabinet behind a stack of linens and pulled out a large garbage bag. Shaking it open, he knelt next to the clothing and jammed the heap into it. He gripped the opening, spinning the bag to prevent any spillage. He tucked it under a cabinet, out of Arabella's sight. He would deal with burning it in the morning.

He moved into the shower and adjusted the water. His palm slammed against the tile wall, and he dropped his head under the hot spray. The water tapped his scalp and ran over his closed eyes and down his body. The tinged water faded clear before he moved a muscle. Any other circumstance, he would be back there assisting his crew in searching the dark and clearing all evidence. Tonight, he'd called in help. The instant he realized Arabella was in danger, he told her not to hang up. He'd hit speaker and grabbed a burner phone that he kept in his car. He barked orders to Conner, and within seconds, her phone was tracked and the coordinates were sent to his car. He refused to consider what may have been If he hadn't reached her so soon.

He shook the water from his head and lifted his chin, scrubbing his beard. He needed to get back to her. His brothers, along with Dawson and Tucker, would have the area cleared and any details taken care of by morning. He twisted the knob and grabbed a towel. Wiping away the beads of water from his body, he cast one last glance around the room. All clear. He flipped the light switch and turned away.

Arabella was still curled on her side when he returned to the bed. He dropped his towel and eased under the covers, wrapped his arm around her, molding himself to her. Her fingers laced with his, pulling his arm tight and giving him the assurance he hadn't realized he needed. They would be all right.

Jewelz Baxter

Chapter 16

Ellis hadn't slept much that night. As he held Arabella, he realized how close he'd come to losing her. Something he never wanted to experience again. He had refused until now to admit, even to himself, the true reason he wanted her here. No, it may have begun as a want, a desire, but having her with him now had become a need. He needed her here. In his home. In his bed. Trading insults and personal jabs across the fence had intrigued him. He had not intimidated her as he had so many others. Her beauty enticed him to desire more. Now, he had spent time with her. Gotten to know her. Tasted her. Letting her go was no longer an option. It would kill him. He needed her beside him.

Arabella had become his only weakness. He could not afford another. Love made people weak. That was what had been drilled into him since childhood. No. No "L" word in this relationship. He was not weak, and neither was she. They were a team and would remain so.

The moon hadn't faded from sight when he rose and moved onto the balcony. He slid closed the door and turned to lean against the railing. His focus pinned to Arabella still sleeping in his bed, he called Conner.

"You two alright?" Conner answered.

"She's sleeping. Meet here at sun-up."

"Not that I'm an expert, but how are you going to manage business while comforting a woman?"

"She's stronger than you realize. But I have that covered also. We're having breakfast by the pool."

"I'll pick up Alex and be there."

"Done." Ellis ended the call and cocked his head, studying Arabella a moment longer. How would she react when she awoke? He blew out a breath and raised his phone again. Surely, it wasn't too early for

Bartel to be up. He tapped call on the screen but had to cut that call short when he noticed her become restless. He quickly recited his request, promising details at a more convenient time, and ended that call.

Quietly, he returned to bed, whispering encouragement as he pulled her back into his arms. It took several moments for her to settle into a deep sleep free of the apparent nightmare. He noted the time and eased from the bed for the second time. About an hour until daylight and he had things to do. He grabbed a pair of pajama pants from a drawer and pulled them on as he walked into the bathroom. He retrieved the bag of clothes and tossed it over the balcony. Checking on Arabella as he passed, he made his way down the stairs and outside. Next to the back door, he pushed his feet into rubber boots, then grabbed the bag and walked to a firepit at the end of the house. He made quick work of lighting and managing the fire. Orange streaks lined the horizon when he decided the contents were no longer identifiable and the firepit was at a point to be left alone.

Back inside, he cleaned the dusty trail from the door to the bath and returned to his room. The sun was spilling through the balcony door when he heard a gasp from Arabella. Her face transformed from an agonizing pain when she inhaled into a relaxed peacefulness.

She smiled and snuggled deep into his pillow.

The sight brought a smile to his lips, and he stepped between her and the blinding rays and settled onto the mattress's edge. "How are you feeling?" He combed her hair away from her shoulder. The bruise on her cheek punched his gut.

"Like I've been trampled guarding the feed trough."

Ellis barked with laughter.

"I love that," she whispered.

He pulled in his laughter to a low chuckle. "What?"

"Your laugh. I'm in pain and you laugh for the first time."

Laughter spilled from him again. "I laugh."

"Not that I've heard."

"We'll change that. I have something to take care of, and then I'll be back up for you. Do you feel like dressing?"

She rolled her head to view his pajama-covered legs then back to his face. "Do *you* feel like dressing?"

He grinned. "I'll hurry back, and we'll dress each other."

"You actually think you can put clothes on me rather than removing them?"

"Is that sass I detect? Perhaps you require a bit of discipline to begin your day?"

"I definitely don't believe I could fight you on that this morning. So, I'll take a raincheck on that, thank you."

Her cheesy grin did nothing to disguise the pain in her eyes. "You never fight me. But raincheck granted. I'll get you something to ease the soreness."

He left her and jogged down the stairs and toward the kitchen when movement outside urged him to change his direction. Through the back door, he met Bartel under the veranda. "Good morning, sir. You don't know how I hated to make that call so early this morning."

"Your brother filled me in." He hung his head, shaking it slowly. "I should have been there. I should have never left her alone. Not even for a minute."

"Don't blame yourself. This happened on my watch, but be assured she's safe from any more threat now."

Bartel nodded. "How is she?"

"Still resting. She'll be down soon."

Mr. Bartel held up a box. "I brought some breakfast."

Ellis gave a nod. "Appreciate it. Hope you brought enough for yourself."

He grinned. "Figured there'd be more arriving too."

Ellis chuckled and clamped his hand on Bartel's shoulder. "Aren't you the unassuming country boy?"

"Got the cow to prove it." He cocked his head toward Burger King nibbling on grass across the yard. "Marshmallows?"

Bartel lifted them from the box.

"I'll go get her."

He disappeared back inside and with a quick trip through the kitchen, he found a bottle of something to better help her stiffness. He took the stairs two at a time and entered his room to find Arabella still curled under the covers.

"Time to get up, Princess." He flipped back the covers and clenched his jaw. His fist squeezing the bottle he held, he dropped next to her. Gently, he touched each bruise. Her hip. Her leg. Both arms. He was nearly vibrating, wishing he could kill D'Angelo again.

"Your cheek looks better." Her fingertip grazed the spot where he'd bled the night before. "How does it feel?"

He caught her hand and brought it to his lips. "Don't fret a moment over me. I would take all this from you and suffer more to keep you unharmed."

"This wasn't your fault."

"I should have been there. I should have said no when you wanted to visit."

"That man was insane. He could have come after me at another time or done something much worse. You're the reason I'm here now. And I don't know how you found me so fast, but I'm thankful that you did."

He smiled. Or at least he tried to put on a smile, knowing that he failed to hunt down D'Angelo before anything happened. A mistake that would never happen again. Any hint of a possible threat against his Arabella would die on sight. "That's because you obeyed me."

She raised her brows, twisting her lips.

"You didn't hang up."

She sucked in a breath and her eyes widened. "I lost my phone."

"We'll get you another." He offered his hand to assist her up.

Her smile was trusting as she placed her palm in his moving to her feet. Her fingers slid between his as she walked with him into the bathroom. He filled her a glass of water for the pain pill before they dressed together. Ellis dressed in his usual suit pants and shirt, while she decided on a mid-calf-length dress to hide what she could of the experience while not putting pressure on the bruises.

"Why are we heading outside?"

"A little surprise." He opened the door and swung his arm for her to lead.

She stepped through and jerked back, her eyes as wide as a kid on Christmas morning.

"He can't open the bag himself."

Arabella whirled back and grabbed the bag of marshmallows from the table and ran past the pool. An awkward lope, but he couldn't take his eyes from her. Her excitement was contagious. He swore that bull ran toward her just as fast. She threw her arms around her pet, and he couldn't hear what she said but he watched her carry on a conversation with her father and that bovine.

"You know you'll have cow shit in your yard now." Alex walked past and fell into a chair.

"Yeah." He acknowledged his brother's remark without losing sight of Arabella.

"Next, you'll have pigs and goats. Close a door and open a window and there you have a chicken coop. You can gather eggs without leaving the house."

Conner laughed and filled the seat next to Alex.

"Burger King is not staying."

"Burger King?" Alex's head fell to the side, his eyes wide. "What happened to 'that bovine won't set one hoof on my property'?

"Don't mind the kid. He's still growing up. She's worth it. I understand." Conner kicked the chair across from him away from the table for Ellis to sit. "You said you had her occupied. I admit this is not what I imagined, but it works."

Ellis dropped into the chair. "All clear?"

Conner and Alex exchanged glances, then Conner pinned Ellis with a curious look. "Didn't you drag the body into the bayou?"

Ellis leaned forward, resting his arms on the table. "No. I put Arabella in the car and got her the hell out of there."

"When your car pinged, it was moving. I rerouted Alex to get me to clean up together."

Ellis leaned even closer to the center of the table. "You didn't take the shot?"

Alex shook his head.

Ellis rolled his head toward Conner, who threw up a hand.

"Not me."

Alex dropped his ankle from his knee and leaned forward, resting his arms there instead. "What are you saying, boss?"

"I had it pressed in his throat, but his head spattered before my trigger clicked. I left him."

"Sure it took?" Alex asked.

"Between the eyes," Ellis confirmed.

A heavy silence fell over the table for a long moment. Ellis pulled in a deep breath and blew it out.

"Lupo?" Conner suggested. "Possible he had a bead on him. D'Angelo was on his list too."

Ellis nodded slowly. "That must be the case. You say the place was clean?"

"Drag marks and tire ruts," Conner explained. "To the untrained eye, it appeared like an ordinary loss of control accident. We covered the drags and searched for any identifiable debris. Nothing."

"No one person alone could have cleared the scene that quick. That SUV would have to be pulled out."

"That's a good sign it was Lupo," Conner announced. "What about her?" He jerked his head toward the direction where Arabella stood talking with her father.

"She understands the severity of the situation."

"You do understand this will define your true relationship with her." Conner's voice was firm and authoritative as he drilled Ellis with an unwelcomed look.

If Conner was attempting to intimidate, he failed. But Ellis appreciated the meaning behind his brother's words. And he was totally on point. Times like this determined whether a woman remained or disappeared. Arabella was going nowhere. "I'm taking her away somewhere for the next week."

"I may take a trip over to Conroe and pay Blake a visit." Alex leaned back and lifted an ankle to rest on his knee again. "She has a signing event there."

Ellis rolled his head toward Alex. "A signing?"

Alex pulled his phone from his pocket. "Yeah. She's really excited about it." He scrolled and held the device out to Ellis. "This is it. Motorcycles, Mobsters, and Mayhem."

Conner cocked his head. "What is that?"

"Apparently, a bunch of authors gather where readers can visit and meet them and purchase books."

Ellis scrolled through the posts, taking in the information and wondering what the draw was. He couldn't comprehend the excitement, but that wasn't important. "Can you get tickets for this thing?"

Alex grinned and retrieved his phone, immediately typing a message. "What you thinking?"

"The lake house is a perfect place to heal and relax."

"We can make a week of it," Alex suggested.

"Alone," Ellis snapped.

"Now, what fun would that be?"

Ellis narrowed a glare at his brother. "I intend to find out just that."

A flash of something through the kitchen window sent a ray of light across the glass top table. Ellis twisted to identify the movement. "Excuse me for a moment." He stood and strolled inside.

"Good morning, Mrs. Moretti. Everything alright?"

She hung her purse on the hook he'd learned she used regularly and turned toward him. "Of course, it is. I guess my old age is creeping in." She laughed. "Just one of those days that takes a bit longer to get going. Arthritis and such. I apologize if I've put you out."

His gaze fell to the dish on the countertop. "You don't punch a time clock. If you need a day off, you know that's no problem. What's this?" He lifted Arabella's phone from the dish and turned it on.

Mrs. Moretti moved to the drawer where she kept her apron and began tying it around her waist. "It was sitting on your steps when I arrived. But I see everyone is outside. You must not have heard it being delivered."

Ellis knew if the doorbell rang, it would have sounded by the pool. Plus, he would have been notified by the security app on his watch. "I'm sure that's it. We've had a lively morning. Why don't you join us on the veranda for breakfast?"

"Oh heavens! And give you even more reason to dismiss me? I'm hardly needed around here anymore with that sweet darling of a girl you have here."

Ellis chuckled. "Mrs. Moretti, you've become just as much a part of this family. You're going nowhere." He grinned. "Remember, you know too much."

"Oh, psh." She batted a hand his way. "Well, in that case, I'll take you up on that. Are we celebrating something?"

"No. Just another morning in chaos."

Mrs. Moretti laughed as she strolled toward the door.

Ellis lifted the item wrapped in brown paper from the dish in question. He reached in and pulled out a mud-spattered license plate. He hesitated a moment, studying it, then flipped it over. 'DESTROYED' was printed across the back in big bold letters. He slid it back into hiding and walked outside.

Conner and Alex were still where he left them. Mrs. Moretti had joined Arabella and her father but keeping her distance from the large animal. He swallowed a smile as he strolled toward the table to take the same seat he'd abandoned minutes earlier.

"Take a look in here." He held out the brown wrapper.

Alex pulled back a side and raised a brow, then handed it off to Conner. He also lifted a corner and gave a slight nod. Then he eased it to the side to read the back. "Mystery solved." He covered the metal plate back and slipped it into the seat next to his leg.

Alex pulled out his phone. "She said, 'Sure. I got you four tickets.'" He threw his head to the side, grinning at Ellis and Conner. "It's a date. Conner and I'll be scarce. You'll barely know we're there."

"Target down. Bikinis on the water in sight," Conner confirmed. "Now what?"

He expected nothing less from his brothers. They always had his back. Mainly because they knew he preferred to be alone, and it irritated him. But they were family, and family was everything. "We eat." Ellis pushed to his feet.

His eyes never strayed from Arabella as he moved toward her. Her excitement reminded him of a kid bringing home their first puppy. The petting and talking to the animal and sharing snacks as if the animal was a best friend. That was the rumor he'd heard also, that dogs were a kid's best friend. Something he wouldn't know since he was never allowed a pet.

Arabella held out a marshmallow to Ellis. He glanced toward it and raised a brow.

She lifted his hand and placed the large sticky puff in his palm. "Just hold it up."

"Did we not have a conversation about bovine spittle yesterday?"

Her eyes glistened when she cocked her head. "We did. Now, feed him."

He vaguely registered a chuckle from Bartel next to him as he narrowed his eyes on Arabella.

"You're always doing for me. This is my gift to you."

"Please explain how sticking my hand into a beast's mouth is a gift."

"It's a new experience, and that's how we grow."

Now was the time she chose to toss his words back at him. He lifted his hand until the animal smelled the treat and leaned in, wrapping his tongue around the white puff, leaving a wet trail behind. "Happy?"

Her smile was beautiful. Correction. She was beautiful. Even the bluing spot on her cheek couldn't mar her beauty. "Maybe." She giggled. "You know, you'll have cow poo on your precious grass now." She twisted the half-eaten bag closed and fell into step next to him.

"A problem for the lawn care service."

Her laughter followed him inside, where they washed and returned to the veranda for a celebratory brunch with family.

Jewelz Baxter

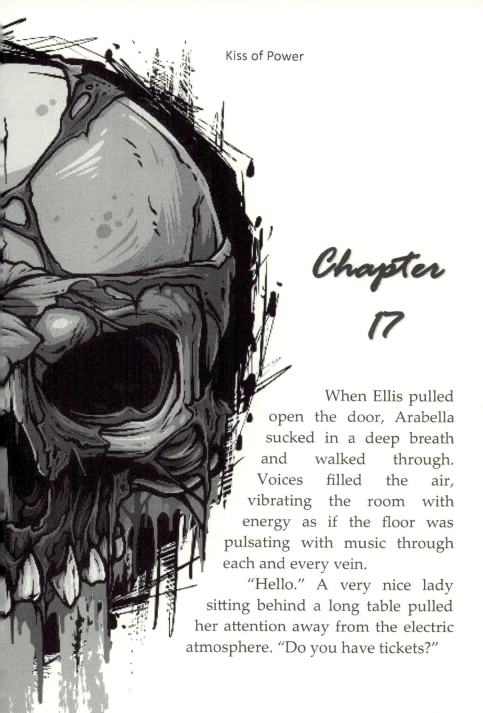

Chapter 17

When Ellis pulled open the door, Arabella sucked in a deep breath and walked through. Voices filled the air, vibrating the room with energy as if the floor was pulsating with music through each and every vein.

"Hello." A very nice lady sitting behind a long table pulled her attention away from the electric atmosphere. "Do you have tickets?"

"Right here." Alex stepped up, offering the woman a printed sheet.

She glanced over the printed paper. "Perfect." She gave a nod to the tall blonde next to her. "You each get a bag. Feel free to take any swag from the tables there as you enter and enjoy your day."

Arabella accepted the bag from Alex and stepped to the table, studying the variety of postcards, pens, and bookmarks. She grabbed a couple of things that caught her eye and dropped them into her bag, which already felt weighed down with books and swag.

A few steps farther in and Arabella stopped. "There are so many people here."

"And we're early. It will only fill up more," Ellis reminded her.

"I don't know where to begin."

"Start at the beginning and go down the line." He held up a credit card. "Buy everything you want. We'll be right here. Fill up that bag then come get another one."

Arabella turned toward the nearest author table. The attractive book display drew her in. The author's eager smile should have been encouraging. Instead, standing face to face with an admired author made her lightheaded, closing out the world around her. She returned the smile and was sure she said hello. Or did she? She could feel the heat rising in her chest. The woman's voice faded as if she were staring at a silent movie.

The author whose name escaped her at the moment reached to a stack of papers behind her. "How about a poster?" Her movements seemed to return the volume to the world around them. "Take a swag bag too."

"Thank you." Heat filled her, threatening her breath as she dropped the small organza bag into the VIP bag hanging over her shoulder. Taking care not to mangle the bare-chested man in her shaky hands, she turned back toward Ellis.

In a flash, Ellis was inches from her, his voice calming her. "What's wrong?"

"I can't do this. I'm a mess."

His eyes narrowed on hers, but no judgement spilled from them. "What are you talking about? I've never known anyone to ever intimidate you. Not even me."

"But I've read their books, at least some of them. Their minds are amazing, filled with worlds no one else could imagine."

Ellis chuckled and glanced over his shoulder toward his brothers before urging her back to the very spot that she had stood moments earlier. "She would like the set, and this man," he jerked his head toward Conner, "will take care of it."

"Absolutely." The author pushed a notepad toward Ellis and grabbed a bag from underneath the table as he jotted down Arabella's name. He ripped it from the pad and handed it to Alex, then printed her name once more and turned it back toward the author.

Ellis glanced toward Alex. "Hang on to that for having any books signed." Then he slipped his arm behind Arabella and guided her to the next table. The next encounter transpired somewhat easier as he took the lead in the conversation. She tried to focus on what was being said and follow his lead, but her voice failed her again after hello.

"Breathe," floated past her ear. She gave a nod and looked up. Kristine Allen. Arabella had the author's Royal Bastards MC series on her Kindle.

"Hi. How are you?"

She gathered confidence from Ellis's palm against her back. "Hello. I love your stories."

"Oh, thank you! Do you have a favorite?"

Arabella's eyes grew. Her brain must have stayed outside the building. "All of them?"

Kristine laughed.

"I mean, I love Venom," Arabella corrected herself, hoping she appeared normal and not like the ball of heat about to burst into flames.

"Is this your first signing?"

Arabella gave a crooked smile.

"Oh, you're in for a treat," Kristine said and stepped around the table. "We need a picture." She moved next to Arabella. "We have a virgin!" she shouted, spurring an eruption of cheers and applause.

Arabella's cheeks burned as she glanced toward Ellis. He was grinning and pulling out his phone.

They posed, and he snapped the photo. She picked out her book choices and moved on as Conner collected and paid for the books.

She stepped toward the next table. Jewelz Baxter. Arabella recognized the Voodoo Troops MC banner hanging from the front of the black table covering, another series she had read.

"Hi," Jewelz greeted her.

"Hello." Arabella scanned the familiar book covers, stopping on one she hadn't seen before. Lifting the book, she glanced up to match the face on the cover to the man standing next to Jewelz.

Jewelz laughed. "Yep, that's Johnny. Finally talked him into being on a cover. Would you like us to sign it?"

"I would love that!"

Ellis moved forward and reached for *Laying Brick*, placing it on the table in front of Arabella. "We need this one also."

Humor filled his voice, causing heat to take root in her chest. She glanced up to catch a wink from Ellis.

"Oh, that's a favorite. I also have special Brick swag I'll add to that," Jewelz offered as she pulled a bag from underneath her table.

"Perfect." Ellis grinned as Arabella still stared at him. "He's a favorite of hers also."

Images of reading that novella together with Ellis flashed through her mind. Great, another thing to trigger her nerves. One thing she'd learned is that Ellis could be a time bomb for inuendoes and subtle touches that others wouldn't notice but that would send her brain on vacation.

Alex stepped up and placed the printed name on the table, and Jewelz personalized the signature in both books, then passed the books on to her hubby to sign. "I hear this is a first for you."

Of course, she did, along with half the people in the building. But Arabella remained silent and nodded.

"My friend, Roux, has just a thing to ease that anxiety." Jewelz motioned for her to step between the tables. "Come with me."

Arabella hesitantly followed Jewelz's lead to see Roux Cantrell. She pulled to a stop, feeling as if her eyes may pop from her head.

"Roux, this is Arabella and she's a bit overwhelmed."

"Oh, girl, I got you covered." Roux reached under her table and pulled out a large bottle filled with an orange liquid and three plastic champagne flutes. "We have mimosas." She began pouring, filling up three glasses, and then lifted one to Arabella and one to Jewelz. "A girl can't drink alone."

Jewelz took her glass. "Absolutely not."

"To a day of bookish mayhem," Roux toasted, and all three women tasted their drink. "Come around here and get some candy too."

Arabella moved around to the front of Roux's table. There on a three-tier stand were the cutest candy bags made of recycled book pages. She accepted the one Roux offered and placed it in her VIP bag. Scanning the books spread out across the table, she noticed a new to her book and chose it. She sipped her drink, focusing on Roux's signature being placed inside the cover.

"Now, let me get that topped off and you can take it with you," Roux offered.

"Thank you so much."

"You know where to find me if you need more." Roux lifted the mimosa container.

The mimosa was doing its job. Well, along with Ellis's constant encouragement. One aisle of authors down and on to the next.

Each table they paused at, she continued to relax, and by the third row of tables, conversations rolled out. They purchased books, snapped photos, and moved on until they reached a display with cover models.

"No books there," Ellis said.

"Are you jealous?"

"These men have nothing on me." He tugged her to collide with his chest, right there amongst the multitude of women hustling from table to table. "I know how to kiss you."

"Maybe I want to do the kissing."

Ellis cocked a brow, and she grinned. He spun her away as if they were dancing and slapped her ass. "Get in line for your photos."

Arabella was enjoying herself. Table after table, author after author, she was loving it. New authors were added to her library and old favorites were bought in paperback. She had no idea how many she'd purchased. She only picked them out while Ellis had sent Conner and Alex out to the SUV twice to empty their load.

Time seemed to speed up as the final aisle of authors stretched out before her. Adrenaline still rushing through every vein in her body, her eyes nearly popped from their sockets. Or so it felt.

Arabella spotted Alex, who had disappeared by the end of the second row of tables. He'd made himself at home behind the table of Blakelynn Hart. The fan girl syndrome was kicking into full gear this time. Every publication Blakelynn had written was permanently ingrained in Arabella's memory. And as this fact echoed through her mind, her brain launched into gear. Ellis and Sebastian, one of Blakelynn's characters, were much alike.

She giggled a little inside. Although she enjoyed the fantasy life of fiction, at times she scoffed at the heroines submitting to their enemies or to such a rude and powerful hero. Yet here she was following their example.

Ellis stepped up and broke the ice, leading them into a lively conversation. A photo was taken and books were piled into a bag.

The announcement counting down the minutes until the doors closed reminded Arabella of the time. It had been a blast once she moved past the mental block. Three authors left and they would call it a day. Darlene Tallman stood behind the next table. Her personality pulled Arabella in and had her talking and laughing as if they were old friends. She scored a set of the Old Ladies Club books. They were new to her, but she had no doubt she would love the heroines.

On to the next, where she walked away with a purple bag filled with Jessa Aarons's books. They were already on her Kindle, but what girl can pass up signed paperbacks of her favorite reads? She peeked inside the bag, smiling at the extra goodies Jessa had dropped in as she moved on to A.R. Hall's display.

A bright new paperback caught her eye on A.R.'s table. Her Mayhem Makers edition. Arabella slowly picked it up. No need to read the blurb, the cover stirred emotions enough on its own. Her mind flashed to the first night she wore the robe of the same green as the color of the title. And the mysterious man filling the cover, something about him brought Ellis to mind. No matter the content of the story, she needed this book. She flashed the cover toward Ellis with a grin. He may have attempted to appear stern, but she noticed the slight roll of his eyes as he stepped forward to pay.

With each author met and more books collected than Arabella had imagined, they turned toward the door. Ellis reached for the two bags she'd looped over her arm. She released one and dug through the other, pulling out the cutest little tin of lip balm she'd collected from Andi Rhodes and tucked it into her pocket. She relinquished the last bag, and he gently guided her back into the fresh lakeside air.

Kiss of Power

Jewelz Baxter

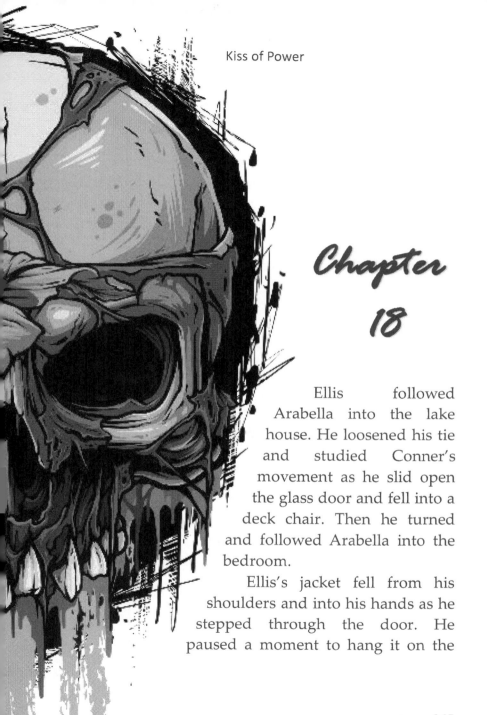

Chapter 18

Ellis followed Arabella into the lake house. He loosened his tie and studied Conner's movement as he slid open the glass door and fell into a deck chair. Then he turned and followed Arabella into the bedroom.

Ellis's jacket fell from his shoulders and into his hands as he stepped through the door. He paused a moment to hang it on the back of a chair as he watched her spin and fall backward onto the bed.

"That was an experience." He moved toward her and lifted one foot at a time, removing her shoes. "You appeared to be enjoying it. Once you realized they're only human, just as you are."

"I don't recall ever being so nervous in my life. Except for . . ." Her words trailed off only to be replaced with a smile.

He stretched out next to her on his side and propped himself on his elbow.

"You're really good to me."

Ellis said nothing, only flashed her a smile.

"You spoil me with very thoughtful surprises."

"Purely for selfish reasons, I assure you." Her eyes met his. He held back the grin he felt from the questions filling those eyes. "It makes me happy to see you smile. Now, tell me what possibly could've intimidated you to your point of anxiety?"

"It was nothing."

"Nothing or no one?"

"It's in the past."

"Not if it upset my princess." Arabella bit her bottom lip. "What happens when you lie?"

Her eyes narrowed into small slits glaring up at him. She folded her arms but said nothing.

"Arabella." His voice was firm and matter-of-fact, reminding her of the consequences.

"You."

"Me?"

"I was terrified when Papa told me I had to spend time as a housekeeper away from the farm. I wondered how he would manage the chores alone. Then here you come, all arrogant and smug, thinking you owned me."

"We've sparred across that fence for years," he reminded her.

"That was different."

"Then maybe I should allow you to punish me."

"I thought I had."

"How did that go?"

"It backfired."

His laugh was deep and warm and felt good inside. She'd told him he rarely laughed, and she'd been right, at least at that time. He hadn't realized until that moment how much she had brought into his life.

"What's going to happen when Papa repays the loan?"

"What have I told you about business?"

"This isn't business. This is my life."

Ellis sobered. "Your father owes me nothing."

Arabella pushed onto her elbows. "What? How could he have paid back such an amount?"

"Business, Princess."

The spark in her eyes faded. Dropping from her elbows, she rolled onto her side. She said nothing more and seemed to be avoiding his gaze.

He combed back her hair. "Hungry?"

She shook her head and reached for his shirt. Her fingers traced a button, round and round and round.

"Are you ready to go home?"

Her shoulder bounced so slightly that if he weren't so focused on her, he would've missed it.

"What did I tell you when I moved you into my home?" She still fiddled with the button as her eyes lifted to his. "You're mine."

Her fingers paused, although the light still evaded her eyes and her expression remained dull.

He zoned in on her blinking eyes. All their fighting and forcing her to rearrange her life, and not even when he disciplined did she shed a tear. The night she feared for her life, tears had surfaced but none fell.

Did the thought of remaining with him repulse her so deeply? He pressed his lips against her forehead and pulled her to him. They had one last night together, then he would take her home if that's what she wanted. He'd wanted her so badly, and he had her, but her words echoed in his mind. It had backfired. Heir or not, her happiness had become more important than his desires.

Ellis had no idea how much time had passed when Alex's voice filled the lake house.

"I come bearing food."

Ellis stood and pulled Arabella to her feet. With their fingers laced together, they emerged from the bedroom. Alex was arranging food containers on the bar. Conner still resembled a statue staring across the rippling water that reflected the evening shades of orange and yellow.

In silence, they filled plates and carried them out onto the deck. Ellis and Arabella settled at the table. Alex handed a plate to Conner and dropped into the chair next to him.

"How crazy was the adrenaline in that place today?" Alex chuckled. "Just from made-up stories people write. You'd think some of those women were meeting rock stars." He shook his head and reached for his drink sitting on the floor next to him. "You'll have to meet Blakelynn when she's not so nervous."

"Nervous?" Arabella blurted, throwing her hand to her throat as if she was choking.

"Yeah." Alex's face twisted. "She's terrified of crowds. I'm proud of how she handled today."

"It's hard to imagine any of them being nervous. They worked the room like champs," Arabella noted, lifting her glass to her lips. "I did have a wonderful time, though."

She glanced up, and Ellis fell into her smile, not as bright as normal but still a genuine smile. The bruises on her face had lightened to be unnoticeable to anyone not searching for them. He reached and squeezed her fingers in response to her silent thank you.

"I want to enjoy the last bit of sunlight on the pier. Want to join me?"

Ellis gave her a nod. "I'll be there before it fades away."

She pushed back her chair and stood. Ellis's eyes feasted on each step she made and the way her hair swayed in rhythm with her hips as she walked. A breeze whooshed across the narrow walkway, ruffling the hem of her dress and offering a peek at her legs. She settled on the end of the pier and dropped her legs over the side before he could pull his focus from her.

"I questioned you showing up here," Ellis admitted to Alex.

"She's having dinner with her author friends tonight. I'll see her in the morning. Thought I'd hang out here a few days. She'll drive me home."

"What happened to him?" Alex jerked his head toward Conner but kept his focus on Ellis.

"Been like that since we returned home," Ellis told him.

"Hey." Alex punched Conner's shoulder.

"I saw Cadence today."

"What happened?" Alex asked.

Conner rolled his head toward them. "Nothing. She was with friends. Stopped cold when she noticed me by the SUV."

"And?" Alex urged.

"She got in her car and left."

Alex shook his head. "That's tough, brother. I thought that was passed."

"Yeah" was Conner's only response.

Alex glanced toward Ellis, bringing his attention back to him. "Brownie points racked up for a while?"

Ellis barked a laugh. "I believe she's homesick."

Alex shot him a look. "She knows there's no reason to stay any longer."

"Does she know that you brought her to stay for her protection?"

Ellis shook his head. "It was best this way."

"True."

Water lapped against the wooden dock, replacing the sound of conversation. Ellis studied Arabella as she sat slumped. Her legs dangled out of sight, no doubt her toes dipped into the cool lake, sending ripples out in circles. A minute or so later, she jerked straight as a statue and, for a long moment, didn't budge.

He liked to taunt her that he knew her better than she knew herself. And he had learned her telltale signs and reactions. But she had stumped him today. He never expected her to be unhappy or want to return home.

Arabella jumped to her feet and spun toward the house, leaving wet footprints that faded as she walked.

"Yes, ma'am?" Ellis looked up as she stood over him. Her smile had returned larger than before.

"You asked me if I remember our conversation that first day."

"I recall."

"But do you remember?"

"I do."

"I want one."

Quickly, he ran through the details of the conversation. His lips twitched, but he forced his features to reveal nothing. "Is that a fact?"

"Yes!" Confidence radiated from her, and the sparkle gleamed once again in her eyes.

"Now, why would you think that?"

"Because then you can't pawn me off just because I'm not an asset anymore."

"You think I'm sending you back to the farm?"

"You said yourself, my father no longer owes you. I've figured out that I was the leverage for that payment, and you said I was going home."

He was unable to control the surprised relief filling him. "Alex, when did Miss Bartel's father fulfill his contract?"

"If I recall correctly, about a week ago."

Her chin dropped.

"Sorry to disappoint, Princess, but the farm is no longer your home. Need I remind you that you're mine?"

"Oh."

"Now, as for your request, do you require a ring or a library?"

"I suggest a ring," Alex spoke up. "Throw a book in front of her and, from what I saw today, she may forget you exist."

"Point taken. Ring it is." He cocked his head toward Arabella.

"Now, wait a minute. You planned on deceiving me?" Her hands popped onto her hips. "Maybe I want to move back to the farm."

"No chance of that."

He couldn't help but notice her breasts lift when she folded her arms underneath them.

"Stop staring at my boobs."

"They're mine, I can stare all I want."

"You have no papers on them or me."

"Need I remind you? I don't need papers. I know who you belong to."

"Well, maybe I do."

"Then, when you ask the question, I'll present the ring." Her beautiful honey eyes rolled with a shake of her head. "You want to see the ring?"

"I know you don't have a ring."

"You just don't know how long I've had a ring."

"Yeah, right."

"Are you sassing me?" He narrowed his eyes. "In the presence of others, you attempt to argue with me?" He slammed his hands onto the chair arms and leaned forward.

Arabella squealed and fled inside in laughter.

Ellis stood and stretched his arms, then unbuckled his belt. "Excuse me. I have an argument to win." He jerked the belt from its loops and strolled into the house.

He walked into the bedroom and closed the door behind him. His hands wrapped around each end of the length of leather as he moved toward where she sat on the side of the bed.

Her spirit had faded. Her smile had not made it into the bedroom.

He moved forward.

"I'll throw an eagle at you if you try it," she warned.

As he'd promised, he dropped the belt on the end of the bed and moved toward her. "Move over." He sat on the mattress, stretching out his legs as his back pressed into the headboard. Her knees touched his legs while she sat cross-legged facing him. He slipped a hand under her skirt, resting it on her leg and bringing her attention to him.

"Well, that was easy."

"I never want to hurt you. I told you the use of that word relays the severity of your need. Now, tell me what I can do."

Her gaze dropped to her lap as she cleared her throat.

Ellis felt his chest tighten. Never had he seen her at a loss for words. His fingers pressed into her soft skin. He was not one for intimacy or encouragement, but he hoped this slight squeeze would relay to her what he couldn't.

"Ah, uh . . . I'm . . ." Her shoulder bounced, and she sighed. "I'm a bit confused."

"Confused?" Arabella remained focused on her lap as she nodded. "You now have me confused."

Her head shot up.

He searched her eyes for answers, but he found none. Intimate conversations were foreign to him. Sharing feelings and understanding others crossed the line. Other than his brothers, he had never discussed such. He had never encountered another whose feelings mattered to him. His mind darted back to the lines she'd obviously stepped across for him. And at one time, he was positive she would have rather slit his throat if it had been her nature.

"Come here." He released her leg and held out his arm for her to move next to him. He waited until she was tucked against his side to step from his comfort zone. "Tell me what has that pretty head of yours spinning."

"Before we came here, you were, well, you. Now, you're not."

"You still have me at a disadvantage. I change for no one."

"Then I've done something wrong, and I don't know what."

"Now, what would make you think that?"

"You haven't tried to touch me since coming here. Now, I know you say you have no reason to keep me for collateral, and I admit that I hated the situation at first, but you grew on me and made me feel special."

The tightness that had gripped Ellis's chest lightened. "I grew on you, huh?"

"Don't get me started on that."

There was that sass he so enjoyed. He grinned, and although he knew she couldn't see his amusement, he prodded more. "When did that happen?"

"What's that matter?"

"Just wondering what sent you over the edge. Was it before or after I so-called shoved my tongue down your throat?"

Her elbow dug into his side as her body jerked against him. "I still hate you."

"Good to know. It would be a shame for you to enjoy being pampered and protected. Not to mention the loss of being tossed over my knee for the occasional attitude adjustment."

Arabella jerked and twisted to sit on her knees and punched his stomach.

Ellis chuckled, then threw up a hand. "All right." Her eyes were still filled with questions, which forced him to admit his failures. "I haven't touched you because I see the bruises and see you flinch in pain. I know nothing of being tender. I've desired to be inside you each night, lying here next to you. It would gut me to know I've added to that pain."

"You've never hurt me," she whispered as if she was afraid to speak.

"I've noticed the bruises on your wrists that you've tried to hide. And your neck."

She straightened, her fingers lifting to touch her throat. "The throat was an accident. You didn't do that consciously. The wrists have never hurt."

I can't do gentle, Arabella. It's not in me. I don't know how to love, so I can't give you that either. The best I can offer is to give you a comfortable life and a promise to monitor the pain." He studied her eyes, ready to evaluate her response.

She returned his stare for a long moment before throwing a leg over his and straddling his lap. Her eyes softened as her hand shot an unexpected warmth through the shirt he wore.

"That's not true. Not wanting to hurt me is a gentleness. Stepping from your comfort zone to give me today is love. And until you understand you have it inside you, I have enough for the both of us."

Her hands slid up his chest and stopped at the topmost button. He could feel his heart pounding inside him. His mind cleared, focusing only on one button after the other being undone. Arabella had never initiated any type of physical contact before. He searched for a reaction, for a comment, but nothing came. He fell into her eyes as she smiled into his.

Her hands warmed his skin, and her fingers combed through the light curls there. "Let me show you how easy love can be."

***

Arabella searched his eyes. There was no resistance there. No condemnation for her taking the lead. All she saw was trust as his eyes remained glued to hers. His shirt easily slipped from underneath his waistband and fell open to his sides. She leaned forward, pressing her lips to his, savoring the slow sweetness of the kiss. Heat from his chest burned into her fingertips as they danced through the thick curls there. Her body began to warm as if she was basking in the hot summer sun. She straightened, catching her breath, and reached for his chin. The coarse hair sent chills up her arms and straight to her core. Forcing her fingers from his beard, she reached, catching his shirt with her fingers and guiding it over his shoulders and down his arms as her palms caressed each rigid muscle they passed.

His cock began to press into her softness, and she smiled. Satisfaction bubbled up that she had gained that reaction on her own terms. Wiggling her bottom, she scooted backward to reach the button and zipper. Her heart pounded against her chest, and in a blur, Ellis was naked under her. She fell forward, and their tongues began a battle for control. His cock throbbed against her thin panties, and his hands wrapped her waist, holding her in place, his fingertips digging into her sides.

A gasp filled her lungs when she pulled away and jerked the belt from where it lay on the bed behind her. She grinned and, as quick as she could, bound his hands from digging into her flesh. He said nothing as she raised his arms, placing his hands behind his head. "You don't get that today. Just enjoy."

Slowly, she lifted her dress over her head and dropped it onto the bed. His eyes never strayed and hers remained focused on his as she reached behind her to remove her bra. It landed with the dress before the panties joined the pile. Slowly, she explored every muscle, from his feet to his neck, peppering kisses along the way, her nipples pebbling harder with each brush across his skin. Her tongue darted out, flicking the head of his cock and swirling around the smooth skin before licking a trail to his side. Her teeth nipped him.

"That's it." His hands, still bound, shot to her head, tangling in the strands and pulling her to him.

Pain pierced her scalp. "I'm doing this."

"Oh, you did this." He brought her lips back to his cock, precum coating the tip.

Her tongue darted from between her smile, licking it away. She cut her eyes toward him, and he pulled her up.

"Now, get up here and ride it," he ground out, the prickling sting fading from her scalp.

"Maybe I'm not ready just yet," she teased.

"That wet pussy straddling my leg says you are."

His voice sent shockwaves through her. And the heated smirk he watched her with as she ground her clit into his knee burned straight to her pussy. Her lips parted, and her tongue glided across her bottom lip.

His nostrils flared. "Princess."

Arabella shuttered, soaking his skin. Her heart raced as she fumbled with the belt and moved higher, frantic to feel his hands on her and him inside of her. The belt flew out of sight, and she slid down onto him, meeting his rising hips. She could feel her muscles tightening around his shaft, igniting a ripple of pure ecstasy. Building and building until it exploded, bursting out with a scream that he muffled by devouring her mouth. He stiffened, his fingers digging into her hips, holding her firm as he filled her.

His grip softened, and she collapsed against him. She lay sprawled over his body, exhausted, becoming hypnotized by the touch of his hand gently gliding over her back again and again.

Ellis jerked back the covers and maneuvered them, tossing the sheet over them both, never releasing her and not uttering a sound.

Arabella snuggled deeper into his side, and as her hand snaked around Ellis, she let her eyelids drift closed. He may call her a brazen hussy again and tease her for her boldness tomorrow morning. Her lips lifted. She didn't care. At least they would be together for him to tease her. The fear from earlier had unnerved her. She should have been glad at the thought of moving out and away from him. But instead, the idea frightened her.

She had come to look forward to their time together when he wasn't working. Even the times they sat silent in the same room, it was a comfort to be near him. Yes, he was rough at times, but he was at times sweet, even if he thought he wasn't. She loved teasing him and watching for a reaction. Usually, her sass landed her in trouble, but it was worth it. She loved the way things had unexpectedly progressed. She sighed, her mind filling with images of Ellis. She loved his eyes—the unusual color, the way they seemed to see into her soul, to hypnotize her. And the rare times he laughed filled her with joy. She loved it. She loved—

Her eyes popped open, and she jerked up her chin. His eyes were hidden, his features calm. She lifted her hand to his cheek, letting it slide down to rest on his chest. He breathed deep and placed a hand over hers. She rolled her head back against his shoulder. He was right. This was her home. He was her home. Because she loved it. And yes, she did love him.

Kiss of Power

Jewelz Baxter

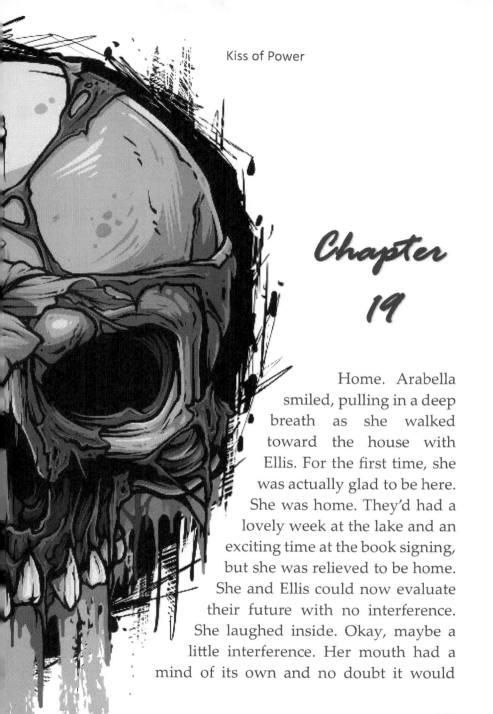

Chapter 19

Home. Arabella smiled, pulling in a deep breath as she walked toward the house with Ellis. For the first time, she was actually glad to be here. She was home. They'd had a lovely week at the lake and an exciting time at the book signing, but she was relieved to be home. She and Ellis could now evaluate their future with no interference. She laughed inside. Okay, maybe a little interference. Her mouth had a mind of its own and no doubt it would control her and spit out something to test Ellis. But then again, he seemed to thrive on that.

One more inhale of the sweet scent of the blooming flowers and she followed Ellis up the steps.

"Conner and I will get the bags. Go on and get comfortable."

She stepped past him, nearly skipping to the stairs that she felt as if she floated up. She was ready to kick off her heels and decide where to store all the books she brought home. Pushing open her bedroom door, she looked inside and froze. Time slowed as she eased across the threshold. Her pink gingham pillow that filled the seat of the large, overstuffed chair in the corner and a family photo were the only signs that she'd spent the last few months here. She stepped to the center of the room where a bed had been the day they'd set out for the lake house. A slow spin made her dizzier than she should have been.

Ellis appeared in the center of the doors that connected the two rooms. "Come with me."

Her stomach plummeted and she struggled to focus on him when he turned away. She stiffened her back and followed.

"I have something for you." He slid open the panel that hid the closet and walked inside.

Arabella eased into the space to find him pulling a long, slender box from a drawer.

"I had this made for you. You want a ring, here are many rings." He flipped open the case.

She stepped next to him. A beautiful gold link bracelet glistened in the light.

"This is our family crest." He pointed out the intricately engraved solid link. "This one is a one-of-a-kind specific only to you and me."

She focused on the ruby lips embedded in the only other solid link. "This is beautiful." She lifted her eyes to his, the blue of them so bright, she couldn't look away.

"You have a question in those eyes."

"You kick me out and smooth it over with an expensive gift?"

"Do I shake you up that much? Princess, turn around."

Arabella's brows furrowed as she narrowed in on Ellis, keeping him in sight until she had swiveled too far to comfortably glare at him. She straightened, her eyes bulging when she saw it, and her pulse raced. Did she dare believe?

"What will it take to convince you? I didn't move you out, I moved you in. Permanently. As it should be."

She stepped forward, running a hand over her clothes hanging in the opposite bay from his. She whirled back.

"I only require a small amount of space. The rest is yours to organize how you please."

"He's here!" Conner's voice sounded far away as he called from the bedroom.

"We have a guest," Ellis confirmed and flipped the box closed. "Are you ready?"

"Maybe," she laughed. He'd taken her by surprise, but he was good at that. She watched as he lifted the box holding the jewelry and walked out with him. Never would she have thought this was where she would want to be. And months earlier, she had fought the need to be here.

Most little girls dream of marrying the perfect man and living happily ever after. How much dreams change over time, she thought. Ellis had all but said he would never marry her, and he was not perfect, but neither was she. And a happily ever after was not the same ideal she had once believed it to be. Life was life, and life was tough at times but rewarding.

She glanced toward Ellis moving from the bottom stair. Fairy tales were overrated.

Ellis stepped forward and spoke to Conner and a man she'd not met before. She remained on the first step, waiting for instruction of what he expected from her. A moment later, he twisted and held out his hand. She stepped to him, dropping her hand in his.

"This is Mr. Carlisle," Ellis announced.

The man gave a polite nod. "It's so good to finally meet the lady I had the pleasure of creating this unique piece for."

"Thank you," Arabella greeted him.

"I'm set up in here. If you'll follow me, we'll get started." He turned toward the great room.

Arabella glanced toward Ellis. He only swung his arm wide for her to go before him. She walked in behind the jeweler and paused near Conner until Ellis stepped up and guided her to a seat opposite where the man was settling into a chair across a small portable table.

"Rest your arm right here, and I'll have your bracelet attached in no time."

Have her bracelet attached? She looked to Ellis again, and he nodded toward her right arm. Without question, she lifted it, stretching it across the flat surface.

"This is painless and only takes a few minutes to weld the links together."

Arabella knew she must look uneasy. She could feel her eyes bulging as she watched the man wrap the gold links around her wrist. Ellis said nothing as he stood over her. She ventured a glance toward Conner, who gave a reassuring smile but also remained silent. She returned her attention to the jeweler working, and as he promised, a few minutes later, he was finished, packing up his tools, and collapsing the table.

Ellis's touch to her shoulder was firm, keeping her in her seat when she began to stand. "I'll show them out and be right back."

She nodded her understanding and dropped her focus back to the permanent bracelet she now wore. The light glistened against the diamond-cut designs in the crest, demanding one's attention. The gold links were brightly polished, and when she dropped her arm, it draped perfectly across her hand just below the wrist.

Ellis knelt, facing her before she realized he had returned. "Princess."

She lifted her eyes. "This means a lot."

"More than you can imagine," he confirmed.

"I didn't have a choice, did I?"

A corner of his lips lifted. "No."

"Then I'm glad you didn't go with a shock collar to keep me on the grounds."

Ellis barked with laughter, rising to his feet with Arabella in his arms. "And that spirited sass is why I love you."

THE END

Mayhem Makers World Collaboration

Motorcycles, Mobsters, and Mayhem author event proudly presents The Mayhem Makers Series. These standalone novels are brought to you by several bestselling authors specializing in writing twisted chaos. You'll get all the bikers, mobsters, and dark romance your heart can handle.
Follow us so you never miss a new release, as they can be added in at any time!

Series Link:
https://amzn.to/3Uta7hH

Acknowledgements

I must say how excited I was to get an invitation to be part of the Motorcycles, Mobsters, and Mayhem signing. Then to be accepted into the Mayhem Makers World was the cherry on top.
Thank you so much, Sapphire Knight, for having faith in me.

My first experience at a signing was at MMM in 2019. I attended as a reader, and I recall walking in and being so overwhelmed!
Remember the scene where Arabella entered the signing and blanked out as she met the first author? Well, that was me.
That poster will always have a spot in my office as a reminder of how far I have come.
And a couple tables later, Kristine Allen drug me from my safe little world.
So, a big thank you to Kristine! I have never forgotten that, and now I'm on the other side of that table, chatting with readers.

Thank you to Roux Cantrell,
my signing partner in crime. Not only is she my signing neighbor in the story, but her Mayhem

Makers character made an appearance at Ellis's dinner party.
And a thank you to my author friends who graciously, and without knowing (shh!), agreed to be part of my fictitious signing event.
You know I love y'all and you can drag me over the coals later.
These would be, in order of appearance, Darlene Tallman, Jessa Aarons, A. R. Hall, and Andie Rhodes.

Hugs and kisses to Rebecca Vazquez.
She worked tirelessly on this late in the game to help get the paperbacks ready and delivered on time.
I would be lost without her.
She keeps me straight from beginning to finish, with all my silly questions and random thoughts, then sprinkles all her magical grammar dust over my work to make it shine.

Now for the ones who have been by my side from my experience at MMM as a reader all those years ago and now as a signing author,
Johnny and Johnny.
Yep, hubby and son.
They let me drag them along the first time and have been supporting me ever since. And now, they're assisting in preparing for the big day of MMM '23.

Mr. B. attends each signing as my assistant, and I love the fact that he agreed to be the cover model for this! He's my true hero!!!

But you know what?
You, the readers, are the real reason I'm here. It's a treat for me to meet each and every one of you and to know you enjoy my words. That is why I write, and I strive to give you my best and hopefully add a little something extra to your world.

Love you all!

About the Author

Jewelz Baxter lives with her husband in Louisiana, near their children and grandchildren. She values family and loves spending time with their grandchildren, supporting their sports and hobbies.

Jewelz writes contemporary and MC romance that ranges from sweet to steamy. She believes in love and happy ever afters, no matter the emotional ride it takes to get there. Be assured, she strives to leave her readers satisfied with the happy ending they desire when they close the book.

When not writing or spending time with family, Jewelz can be found on a Harley, exploring the backroads with her husband. She admits this is where many of her stories and characters have been born. While Jewelz has her own bike, she confirms there is nothing like being on the back of a bike, wrapped around her man.

If you'd like to get to know Jewelz better, visit her website, follow her on social media, or sign up for her newsletter. You can find all her information here:
https://linktr.ee/authorjewelzbaxter

Other Books by Jewelz

*Books range from sweet to steamy.
Jewelz allows the characters to decide their boldness as they pull you into the story.

Voodoo Troops MC Series

Silent Chains MC Series

Darby Crime Family Series

Visit Jewelz's website for the most current book list, including anthologies.

www.authorjewelzbaxter.com

Made in the USA
Columbia, SC
27 July 2024